Tonight Only

Tonight Only

Terry Ross Erickson

iUniverse, Inc.

New York Lincoln Shanghai

Tonight Only

iUniverse, Inc.

For information address:
iUniverse, Inc.
2021 Pine Lake Road, Suite 100
Lincoln, NE 68512
www.iuniverse.com

Cover illustration by Carolyn Erickson.

ISBN: 0-595-29641-6

Printed in the United States of America

Contents

TENT UP

Peaceful sweet morning,
    Elephant done have her bath;
Men yellin', "Hebe, hebe,"
    Cynchin' up the tent.
Now elephant standin' in de hay,
    Men restin' from their chant—
Wipin' sweat from their eyes
    From risin' up the tent.

1

Curtis parked our old '57 Chevy school bus on the side of the boulder-strewn hill at Circus Winter Quarters in the San Bernardino foothills. Unfortunately, we listed to the starboard. I reversed the bedding but it made it worse. Now we were slipping into the headboard.

"Don't open the back door, whatever you do!" I yelled. "I'll fall into the bear cage!"

Curtis peeked out the back window. "Look! An elephant just walked by!"

"I hope its tail was down," I said, not believing him. So this was what a real circus was like.

"I can move the bus again if you want me to. There's plenty of room in this field even though people are parked all over the place."

"It's pitch dark out there. I can't see anything but that bread van behind us with the bear. You don't know what's outside, and besides, we have to stay close to the electrical outlet." I could hear the bear moaning softly in his cage.

"I won't run into the elephant, if that's what you mean."

He would move the bus if I insisted, but he already had his pants and shoes off and the bedcovers turned back and I wanted a few minutes to write.

"I'm having trouble sitting in my desk chair. I feel like I'm going to be washed overboard any minute now, just like when I was at sea." I had a way of always bringing up my one and only trip abroad on an ocean liner. For me, that was about all I had for a lifetime to show in the way of adventure and excitement.

"When were you at sea?" he asked. I heard a trace of sarcasm.

He knew what I meant. "When I went to Europe on that luxury liner, of course."

"I can move the bus," he repeated halfheartedly.

"That's all right. It's an adventure to live downhill." I held on to the chair arms. Shadow, our Doberman, swaggered by like a drunken sailor. He looked up at me with pleading eyes. "Maybe later, we'll straighten the bus up," I said, watching the dog struggle uphill toward the front door. "I'd like to type but I can't when the ship's sinking."

We looked at each other and broke out laughing. What was a nice little gray-haired grandma doing, following a one-elephant mud show down the road? Just a few weeks ago, I was living in Houston, and the circus was just a sweet fantasy left over from childhood days.

My hobby was circus. I was an armchair buff who subscribed to the two circus magazines, *Bandwagon* and *Circus Report*, never dreaming I would someday be "circus."

In the December 15, 1981 issue of *Circus Report*, Big John Strong had run an ad for a ticket manager and Pie Car couple. I looked at Curtis after reading the ad to him. "Wouldn't it be exciting if we could do something like that?" I said with stars in my eyes.

"Why not?" he said, pokerfaced. Behind all that gray beard of his, it was difficult telling what kind of an expression it was.

"No way! Neither one of us has ever worked for a circus before."

"We'll never know unless we try." In moments he was dialing directly to Big John Strong's home. Gudrun Strong answered. No, John wasn't there. He was in Indianapolis. She gave Curtis the number at his hotel, but when Curtis called, John wasn't in. He left our phone number and a message for John to call back. John returned the call all right—the next day, only from Cincinnati.

He as much as hired us right then. We were to meet with Hugh Miles in Houston, December 20th, then call John back after Christmas for the final word.

That ad in the *Circus Report* had changed our lives. Circus Report is to the circus world what Billboard is to vaudeville. The ad had said John wanted a man and wife team—an older couple—to manage the ticket window, office and pie wagon. The ad had our name on it as far as dreamy-eyed me was concerned, just what I'd been waiting for.

Years before, when we were living in Willits, California, Big John's "mud show" passed through town. I interviewed Sandy Strong, John's adopted daughter. We talked about doing her father's autobiography while he was still around to tell it. As we visited, I began to soak up the circus atmosphere. What would it be like? Of course, it was impossible. I was fat and forty-ish and had no experience in any form of show business. Nevertheless, I created a fantasy in my mind as I talked to Sandy.

"What's going to happen to the circus if your father retires or...?" I didn't want to say die.

"I don't know. Me and my brother don't know much about running the circus, only working it."

"Curtis and I are—small business consultants," I said with spontaneous manufacture. We were really writers after a story. "Wouldn't it be wonderful if someday we could help you run the circus, teaching you eventually how to take over?"

Sandy nodded as she invited me to the back of her "wagon," which was a large truck with a camper on the back. She and another girl, Czigi, were fixing dinner in a postage stamp-sized kitchen.

"I'm not all that interested in running the circus, but young John is," she said, turning a steak over in a small skillet. "I'd rather be performing. I do birds and dogs."

Later, I would always maintain that I'd planted the idea way back there, and what was to follow was the result. I lost touch with Sandy, but I did write to Czigi at her permanent address in Oregon. I didn't like the man she was with. The first time he gave me a snarling look, I got the message he didn't approve of a towner like me befriending Czigi. I praised her act and made suggestions to how she could improve her it. That's when he really growled. She never answered my letter. Maybe he intercepted it. I wanted very much to make friends with her but she left Big John's show soon after they came through Willits.

We left Northern California, moved to Houston, worked hard, got prosperous, started living "high on the hog," went into debt and ended up having to work twice as hard to support the three bedroom, four bath plus pool Spanish villa we had been dumb enough to lease.

I returned to college and Curtis became founding president of the Houston Professional Translators' Forum. We both wrote a few books, then sat around our 22-foot swimming pool waiting for them to sell. Before publishers courted us with book sales, IRS sniffed us out for back taxes. Like vultures after a rabbit with a broken leg, they filled our mailbox with duns when we were expecting checks from publishers.

Unreal, impractical and way out as it seemed, jumping at the chance to run away with the circus seemed for the moment a delightful escape. Besides, it was bound to reduce our income into a lower bracket.

John had said he liked the gist of us over the phone. He told us to call Gudrun again and tell her to hold the position open. We were to wait for Hugh Miles to bring the Christmas show to Houston. It would be set up on my own college campus near our house for one night only. How was that for service? A circus coming right to my door almost to get me, and if they liked us, we were hired.

Like an audition, we rehearsed our "gig." I told Curtis to be sure to tell Hugh that he knew how to tie knots. Around a circus tent, ropes and knots were very important. But when Curtis met with Hugh Miles, the last thing on his mind was knots. Sunday morning, Curtis went over to the campus alone, dressed to the hilt in his best suit. Just in case they liked his knots, I slipped work clothes into the trunk of the car.

When he arrived at the auditorium, doors were still locked and the circus performers were stomping around outside in the cold. Curtis found the janitor, got the doors open and spent the rest of the day helping them unload and set up. During the second show, he returned home and got me so I could see the third performance. We rushed back, but when we arrived, there was no audience. The huge school auditorium reverberated with empty sound as we took seats in the front row. I heard the door shut. It was the custodian who slumped down in a seat in the last row.

Swami, the Master of Ceremonies, came around and whispered to Curtis, "Have you seen the show?"

"Sure," he answered. "I was here for the first show."

"Has your wife?" He sounded like he hoped I had so they could cancel the final act. Two of the clowns had been hurt in an accident and morale was low.

"No," I said. "He just brought me over."

Swami disappeared back stage.

The drummer rat-tat-tatted his opening, the organist boomed out an introductory circus number and the curtain went up. Swami came out on stage with the microphone and did a monotonal, monologuous mimicry of a fast freight train conversation as he introduced the Widgets. Dressed in fantasy animal costumes, complete with fur faces, they tumbled across stage. The girl animal had light-up titties like a "burlycue" number. One "crittur" had fall-out-of-the-socket eyes. They clowned and tumbled and shot off fake guns, chasing each other around the stage for ten minutes of warm-up.

Swami came back with more machine-gun delivery. He announced a rola bola juggler who balanced on a platform on top of metal cups on top of a rolling cylinder on top of a ball.

Swami's wife, Marsha, did heel drops from an on-the-ground trapeze, which looked like a child's swing.

The Hendricks, who were also the Widgets, came back on, this time in a trampoline act instead of the fur face costumes. Curtis had raved about them all the way over in the car. The father, the mother who looked like a teenager, and the son did a three-person-locked-together somersault, the best I'd ever seen.

I sat there, laughing my fool head off, clapping my hands hard enough for blisters, stomping my feet and yelling loud enough to make up a whole audience.

Now the acts were playing to me alone. Little did I know, my enthusiasm was cinching down the job for us.

No doubt about it, I was the celebrity. Swami went down on one knee like Al Jolson. He threw everything in the pot, crying huge crocodile tears in soulful dirge to an empty house and gratitude for a three-people audience. I think it had now dwindled to two. The custodian was no longer in the last row.

The performers did the finale and Swami invited us up on stage. Taking his hand, I stepped up into the bright lights. The custodian had gone to open the door. A small black family came in late—too late for the show, but nevertheless, they also were invited up on stage. The whole cast paraded by, hugging and squeezing us like old friends.

All too soon, the show was over. I helped disassemble the drums and cymbals. Neil Armstrong, the organist, picked up his music. The drummer, well plastered by now on a bottle of Cognac making the rounds, took his time packing and belting his drum cases shut. I'm sure I must have unscrewed several setscrews not intended to be disturbed, but he smiled graciously through bleary eyes.

At least I could do one thing useful around the circus, if it were only taking drums apart. I felt uneasy about never having worked a circus before. Certainly, John hadn't sent his circus all the way to Houston to entertain the new cook. Or had he?

But I took the bait. We were running away with the circus! From now on, my life would be fun-filled, work-filled, one night stands—a world full of laughter, circus music, the smell of elephant shit, peanuts, cotton candy and a lot more.

2

Out in California, the van that carries the elephant stood, dust-covered, in an open field. Across its broad red side was emblazoned:

THE CIRCUS THAT HAS MORE FRIENDS THAN SANTA CLAUS.

While others were waiting for Santa Claus that Christmas Eve, we were waiting for a big brassy ringmaster and circus owner to give us the gift of our lives. We began packing. We would be catching up with the circus in Banning, California, two thousand miles away on February 26th.

We had just six weeks to break the lease, sell off three extra cars and auction extra furniture we had bought to fill the three bedrooms, living room, den and maid's quarters. We would be leaving behind my Spanish villa, swimming pool, social life, college, the oppressive muggy heat and all that oil that somehow pervaded even the atmosphere and coated everything with a reminder of where Houston's wealth came from. Oil wasn't so glamorous when it was on your clothes, on the windshield and not in the engine or under an oil derrick where it belonged. I would never, under any condition, regret leaving Houston.

We held garage sales, porch sales, patio sales. We ran ads in the paper, pinned notices on bulletin boards at the supermarket and then, finally, paid a neighbor kid to haul off what was left. Our worldly goods diminished, but not enough. All we had was the station wagon and a small pull trailer to move with.

We thought of building sides on the trailer with a roof and turning it into a gypsy wagon. Then I thought, why not a gypsy bus?

"Let's buy an old bus," I said brightly, sure that would solve all our problems.

"What would we do with it?" He wasn't a bit enthusiastic.

"Live in it, of course. They're better'n trailers."

"Where would you find one?"

"I'll watch the newspaper ads." I was miffed at his lack of interest. It was a good idea. I just knew a bus was right for us.

There were tons of ads to scan through. It was almost Christmas. Everyone was selling anything that could be sold, in order to buy more junk. No one would want an old school bus for a Christmas present.

I found it three days before Christmas, which is an unfortunate time for anyone to have a birthday, but Curtis had been born an early Christmas present for the Ericksons.

"Happy Birthday!" I greeted Curtis, shoving the newspaper ad under his nose. "They only want 450 dollars for it. I offered him three bills and he said come and get it."

"I suppose it doesn't run for that price," he said.

It didn't. The next day as the tow truck driver backed the bus onto our driveway, I stood looking apologetically at Curtis and shrugging my shoulders. "Whad'ya expect for three hundred—a Cadillac limousine?"

It was several colors, mostly blue, and the interior smelled of rain-soaked carpets, wet leaves and neglected debris.

"I'll scrub it down," I promised, "then we'll pull the seats out and lay down some insulation and carpet. You'll see. It'll be really nice."

But Curtis wasn't exactly thrilled. The bus hadn't made it under its own steam. Not just any tow truck could tow it, either. We had to wait around all day for the "big tow truck." Among other things, the brakes were gone.

Its previous owners had towed it, riding the clutch all the way because the brakes went out. Besides brakes, it had to have a new clutch plate. It seemed a monumental task to get it roadworthy, and we hadn't officially been hired yet.

However, the day after Christmas, Curtis phoned John Strong. He said the job was still open if we were interested at three hundred fifty a week for the two of us.

Curtis was radiant as he accepted the job and made the final arrangements. I was absolutely slap-happy.

I wrote a song—a circus song that got me in the circus mood. The whole idea of running away with the circus was absolutely fantastic. One thing for sure, I intended to keep it a secret from all of my children. I couldn't stand their ridicule. It would ruin the whole adventure.

I could hear the music in my head—gay, marching, ascended, not descended. It pounded a rhythm in perfect meter. It set a spell, it marched well—Life is a circus!

Life is a circus, a circus,

A gay balloon, a big baboon—

Life is a circus.

A trampoline, a funny scene—

Life is a circus.

A funny clown, another town—

Life is a circus.

Chorus:
It's razzle-dazzle and razz-ma-tazz,

It's sequined tights and summer nights.

Life is a circus, a circus.

A brand new town, tent coming down—

Tent going up! Come fill your cup!

Life is a circus!

I couldn't stop. Each day was a whirling dervish of excitement for both of us. I began writing comedy. My publisher requested a cookbook. I sent him twenty-four pages on how to make spaghetti. I came up with some garlicky dialogue like, "Some recipes call for 1 Tbsp. minced onion, whattadahell you gonna do with the resta da onion? Same for da garlic. Whos's gonna squeeza da cloves of garlic to getta da juice out?"

I was still laughing when the rejection slip came and a short note saying: WE ASKED FOR A COOKBOOK AND YOU SEND US THIS?

But I still wasn't discouraged. The whole thing about the circus had put me in exuberant spirits.

January 3rd, Big John called again. His daughter, Sandy, had been in a wreck, but now she was home. Sandy said she remembered us. I was delighted. It was one more final strand of silk to be woven into the picture. It seemed that my meeting with Big John Strong was inevitable.

Big John Strong had, in the last ten years, brought back to America the romance of over a hundred years ago. Ringling, Barnum and Bailey, now owned by the Felds, played indoor arenas around the whole nation. Major shows like Beatty-Cole have gone indoors too. But Big John with his little traveling tent show played one night stands to oil drillers in Wyoming where the population a year ago was 259, including the coyotes, and now had swelled to over 200 workers and their families.

When asked why the resurgence of circus in America, Big John said, "With so many sports events being shown on TV, wives and mothers are desperate to have a place to take the kids."

I still found it hard to believe. We were going to be part of the circus life, do one-night stands in towns across the West that I hadn't even heard of and entertain oil workers in Wyoming. But back there in the beginning, neither of us questioned the show or just how far it was going to travel.

We were so eager to get going that the days flashed by. I painted the bus a delicate beige pink, called Frivolous Fawn by the company that made it. My oldest son, who is a mechanic, repaired the bus. Now we had brakes and a clutch. He worried about us taking off for California in such an old vehicle, so his parting gift was a fire extinguisher. Then came the day when we pulled out—Curtis, Shadow our dog, and me—with the utility trailer behind, heavily loaded with all our possessions.

Before we traveled half a day, we got pulled over by a Texas cop. He said he flashed his lights at us for five miles before we finally saw him in our mirror. He guided us to a back street of the mean little town. He was a mean little cop, too. Forget what they say about how everything in Texas had to be big.

"You don't have current tags on this h'yea bus or that trailer," he drawled. It was pouring down rain and bitter cold. We had no heater in the bus.

"Get out!" He snarled.

"Her, too?" Curtis said, bewildered.

"No, just you!" I could see the cop's face. He looked meaner'n a street thief robbing an eighty-year-old blind man. He was a far cry from the CHP's in California. Why couldn't they let us get out of Texas without leaving a bad taste in our mouth?

In this case, we were given sixty-two dollars worth of gall to drink. The worst part was him wanting to see our proof of ownership. I panicked looking for the registration. We hadn't had time to change it over into our name. He acted like we had stolen it from the church. I never wanted to see Texas again.

After we passed San Antonio, the weather became increasingly foul. We broke down in Fort Stockton, couldn't find a mechanic and nearly froze to death without a heater or a stove. I didn't mind the cold food, but the cold feet were miserable. I sniffled and moaned with the cold. I worried about my dog. Dobermans don't have all that much fur. I would have put him under the covers but Curtis snarled at him and pulled the covers down tight.

Everything was frozen, including the dog's water. I had all the clothes I could get on—underwear, pajamas, pants, sweater, shirt, second sweater, overcoat, scarf around my neck, another scarf around my head, two pair of socks, fur-lined leather slippers—but still I was cold.

It was snowing outside, the streets were frozen and it just kept getting colder. The dog wouldn't go outside even to toilet. I think the pee just froze up inside of him. I wrapped an old black sweater around him to stop some of the shivering.

Two tow trucks later, we finally crossed the Texas border. We replaced the drive shaft, but every time we had to climb so much as an anthill, we had to drop into granny gear.

The road was long and tiresome. To entertain myself, I thought about the circus and tried to finish the music to my song. I loved the lyrics but the music wasn't coming out right. I could see it now, spreading all over the country. It would start a new fad, a renaissance of circus music. Fashions would respond. Clown outfits and sequined tights would become the rage. Come to think of it, the abbreviated G-strings worn by circus performers wouldn't be such a bad idea. Sequins would be in, as well as stretch leotards, but blue jeans would definitely be passé. It was a silly thought, but I felt buoyantly happy. It was a perfect day for a circus.

It began to dawn on me. I would have a new address now. Even if we would be on the road most of the time, our mail would go to winter quarters in Yucaipa, John Strong's huge sprawling ranch in the San Bernardino Mountains. From there, our mail was to be forwarded to us every week. We had asked John several times about it and he always reassured us that we would get our mail speedily. It was important to us as writers. We had to keep an open line of communication with our publishers.

John's ranch seemed to be a huge nerve network for all his operations. Not only was everyone's mail processed through there, but the ranch served as a supply depot, storage yard and animal training center, as well as their personal home and retreat. I tried to picture in my mind in advance just what it would be like. I was seeing it as a jungle compound with lots of trees and seclusion. After all, they had an elephant. A few years ago, they had a lion.

By 11 A.M., we had crawled up the steep road to the ranch in granny gear. I could have run up faster. It was agonizing to be so close and the bus straining and groaning to get those last few miles. Then there it was! The old two-tone tent stood in a rocky field, the words MAIN ENTRANCE emblazoned across the front and an elephant out back leisurely covering herself with a cloud of hay.

A cowboy twirled a lariat in a wide circle; another man walked a llama on a short leash. A bear ran through a repertoire of tricks. Trailers and vans hung on the side of the hill, parked this way and that, all hooked up by an octopus of electrical cords to one electrical breaker box.

A gorgeous blonde girl strolled by, her hair caught back in a bit of pink georgette. Swinging her hips and wearing faded tight shorts, she wandered from trailer to trailer saying, "Hi."

We parked alongside a small van that belonged to Sandy Strong. She greeted us warmly. I was amazed how much she favored me—enough to be taken for my own daughter. She had put on winter weight, but she was still very pretty.

I already knew that she was John's adopted daughter. I suspected she wasn't too close to chic young Gudrun Strong, her stepmother. Gudrun was something like thirty years younger than Big John, even though she herself had a lovely teenage daughter named Michelle.

I looked forward to getting to know Sandy better. I wanted us to become very close. After all, we were to be with the circus in order to train her to manage it eventually. I'd need her to guide me through those first few days until we knew what we were doing.

From the window of the bus, I could see the two llamas with their doe eyes watching us. Next to us was a caged brown bear in a bread truck. Dogs barked everywhere. Shadow was kept busy answering them and sorting out all the new exotic smells.

Everyone bustled around, busily getting ready for the sneak preview. Big John had invited many of his friends, the nearby town and the Circus Fans of America to see the first show of the season.

But I was disappointed with the afternoon matinee. The acts were ragged and ill-timed, the generator roared noisily, drowning out the canned music and everyone showed their nervousness. Without a live band, the magic and razzmatazz just wasn't there. I remember when we saw the show in Houston. The organist and the drummer put so much added sparkle in the show. Now, instead of the enchanted spectacle that had sold me on circus, I found the show as tarnished and frazzled as Big John's old gold lamé Master of Ceremonies coat.

Plump little Sandy did a fat-lady-on-the-trapeze act without any extra padding. Then she did a fire routine where she wiped a bit of lighter fluid across her hand as if she were really holding fire. But the act fell flat. People wanted to see some real fire eating. Sandy led the little Pygmy goats around. They were cute, but it didn't make an act. Anyone could have pulled them over the hurdles by a leash. The whole show needed more sparkle, but then, this was only a dress rehearsal. It had to get better. Besides, who was I to be a critic? More than anyone else, I was the one who had to get my act together.

3

The following day, the show people spent their time rehearsing and working the rough edges off their acts. Some of the performers had transferred together from Franzen Brothers Circus back east. They formed a clique among themselves. One of them was Marian. She was Sam the clown on the show.

"That's some dog you have there," Marian said, reaching out a hand of friendship to Shadow, my Doberman.

He growled.

"I think he likes you," I said, hopefully. "Are you good with animals?"

"I train some of the show animals, and I have a dog act I work in the ring."

"Maybe you could train Shadow to do something," I said with a sigh, more pleading than complaining. "I'd settle for him learning to walk nicely at my side without pulling me over."

"I'd be glad to walk him," she said, as I quickly handed her the leash before she changed her mind. The last I saw of them, Shadow was pulling Marian uphill about twenty-five miles an hour. When they returned, she handed me his leash very firmly. "He bit me," she scowled.

"What did you do to him?"

"I tried to make him sit down. All I did was push on his behind."

"I doubt if he wanted to sit down. Besides, he's funny about anyone messing with his backside." I saw her hand wasn't bleeding. I couldn't imagine my precious Shadow breaking the skin.

"He could have bit me," she added petulantly. "I think he considered it."

"You'd know if he didn't like you. If he'd bit you, we'd have the only one-armed clown around."

Ignoring Shadow, Marian entered the bus and sat down in his chair. Shadow sniffed in disgust and jumped up on my bed.

Marian had quite a story to pour out. I had the feeling she'd been holding it in for a long time. Slowly, she began unraveling her confused childhood. Like pulling a string on a sweater, the more she tugged, the thinner the garment she used to conceal her identity became. Her parents were violent. She had massive feelings of rejection. In an effort to find her own identity, she had sky-dived, fought forest fires, worked as a lumberjack, and now, as a circus clown. Her "Sam" costume was very clever. I had stared at it for several minutes before I realized the show didn't carry two midgets. Just when I wondered if the midget on the bottom was getting tired of carrying his buddy around on his shoulders, Marian moved a certain way so I could tell that "Sam" was just one person with a doll attached.

Marian seemed to want to attach herself to us from the beginning. But I felt uncomfortable around her. She moved in too fast, playing the most dangerous game of all—being two people, hiding from herself. Sam the clown was happy. But Sam the clown had to be just one of the boys.

Marian was pretty in a plain-faced way, like a barren fog-covered Cape Cod morning. She had a softness about her like a wild young animal, even when she was trying to be tough and hard. Her smoky gray eyes always looked about ready to cry. The sexiest thing about Marian was that suggestion of tears.

Marian had a good figure, prettier than some of the other women on the show, but more athletic and muscled. When Marian walked, she swaggered like a cocky young boy. Only somehow, on Marian, with her full, well-developed breasts and curving hips, it didn't seem boyish.

If I failed to make friends with Marian, I succeeded in impressing the women who ran the storage yard where we had to dump all our extra furniture and possessions we had brought from Texas. Mary and Elaine were sisters who lived together with their whole houseful of children. They invited us to their home because they were fascinated about us joining up with the circus and wanted to hear more.

"I think it's absolutely wonderful, you having the nerve to do something different like that," Elaine said. "I don't know a thing about circuses."

"What does the bear eat?" one of her boys chimed in.

"Vegetables."

"I didn't know that." Elaine was wide-eyed. She quickly gathered all her children around us in a circle. "Their bear is a vegetarian, kids," she explained. I got the idea she was pushing vegetables with them.

"Is that what he wants?" the five year old said suspiciously.

"I don't know what he wants, but if he's hungry, he eats what he gets."

"What does he eat, then?"

"The way it goes," I said, "someone from the circus goes to the local grocers and says, 'have you peeled the produce this morning?' With accurate timing and a glance at his scrap barrel, he just has. Then you say, 'I have a pet.'"

I had the children's attention. "Never tell him it's a bear. Just say, 'I have a pet and he likes scraps.' If you smile, you can usually get a big crate of vegetable peelings and overripe fruit."

"What did the bear eat today?"

"Rotten rutabagas," I said straightfaced. "I guess I didn't smile enough."

It was the last day before opening the season. The tent was taken down and packed up. Nothing went right; everything went wrong. The performers were cross and out of sorts. They were all broke and had opening night jitters. The back yard looked like hurricane country after a big blow, with equipment scattered everywhere, trying to fit this and that into already stuffed vehicles. Some blew off steam by yelling at each other. Even the elephant expressed herself as she swayed back and forth, chomping on her hay. She didn't have much to yell about.

Circus vans were newly painted, the side show trailer was freshly lettered with elaborate art work by a local artist, Ray Brashears. The tent was rolled on its wheel and hay was stored in the large red van.

We requisitioned the butane tanks and range from the side show trailer. It had been gutted to make way for the oddities collection. The butane would come in handy on the road, but I still intended to use all my electric kitchen. After all, the electricity was free. The show carried that huge noisy generator with it.

I was getting tired of waiting for the electricity to come on when Red, the circus manager, came by and said casually, "Oh, you don't have electricity until 3:00 P.M." I learned very quickly that it seldom came on before four, and by that time I had to get ready to go on the door. The only reason the electricity was turned on was to make popcorn for the show.

I considered that to be a disaster, the first of a series of terrible disappointments about traveling with a road show. No electricity meant no double baking pans, no muffins, no steam table and no Mr. Coffeemaker which I had just purchased. Then there was the matter of lights and heat. It was still terribly cold at night. Worst of all was refrigeration. I couldn't possibly run a food car without refrigeration.

I tried to talk to Sandy about it, but already she was strangely uncommunicative. She was so eager to have us on the show the first day. But after that, it was as if ice water had been thrown over her.

While I trusted Curtis to work the matter of power out with the bosses, I went shopping. Certainly there was some mistake. I had understood Big John to say there was plenty of electricity when we talked to him over the phone from Houston.

I spent over a hundred dollars on groceries and came back from the store ready to take on a whole army, or at least a whole hungry circus. Wasn't I the new "Cookie?"

We arrived in Banning ahead of all the other circus vehicles. I had breakfast ready by 11 A.M. By three o'clock in the afternoon, surrounded by stale doughnuts and the aroma of much heated coffee, I sank back in the chair, doughnut in mouth, wondering why I didn't have any customers. I ended up eating most of the bacon, hard-boiling the eggs and hoping the bologna would stay cold enough till I could get some electricity.

Then, all at once I was swamped. I fixed several breakfasts, even sold the stale doughnuts and made my first day's take.

But any joy was shortlived. At 2:00 A.M., I sat freezing in the bus, my only light, three candles—and the generator off. Curtis complained that he was hungry. Silently, I handed him a boiled egg. We had witnessed an evening of many small disasters for the whole show.

First off, the reel truck tried to pull over a hump of sand, only to get stuck. The men hooked a chain under the front bumper, then attached the chain to Neena's leather harness. But the elephant couldn't pull the big truck out. The bumper bent and threatened to come off altogether. Finally, Red dug the wheels out with a shovel.

The next morning, everyone, unaccustomed to the rigorous new schedule, was more tired than ever and crabby.

"We got an eight o'clock performance tonight, so we won't be on the road until ten or eleven. And we have a matinee performance at 1 P.M. tomorrow. That's going to be tight," Curtis said to Red, the circus manager. "How are we going to make it?"

Red smiled. He removed his battered old hat and wiped his brow with the back of his hand. "That's all right. We'll make it easy," he sighed, "somehow."

Curtis had yet to lose his enthusiasm.

"Aren't you interested in being around all these circus people?" He watched Tina sashaying across the lot. Tina was built. Besides being an acrobat, she was also the animal trainer and shoveler of elephant waste products.

"Nope," I said, ignoring his oogling. "Half of them aren't even dry behind the ears." I would later learn that the youngest was often the wisest, and the dumbest—far more intelligent than to be expected on that little show.

Meanwhile, as I sized them up, I was getting sized up myself. I didn't know yet that as "first of May," we wouldn't be accepted as being "circus" during the first season. We were still enjoying ourselves with all the zeal of a four year old at his first circus.

We loved the night driving more than anything else, but sometimes, in the depth of night, were weren't all too sure where we were.

"Are you positive that we aren't parked on a railroad track?"

"Of course not," Curtis answered back, miffed.

"Then how come that train is vibrating the whole bus until my teeth rattle?"

"It's heavily loaded…probably five engines to get over the pass. Haven't you heard the old saying—subtle as a freight train?"

Leave it to Curtis to give a technical report while parked for the night on a train track.

4

Each day, we got to know the show better. At first, there was the usual trying to match the name with the performer. Everyone knew Big John. When he walked on the lot, there was no mistaking that he was their leader. He was flocked around like a teenage idol, his people looked at him reverently, and standing a head above everyone with that Barnum look about him—the oversized head, the snow-white hair, the prominent forehead, the deep-set eyes—he clearly took his place as the most flamboyant ringmaster left in the circus.

I wanted to do Big John's biography, but he frightened me. I couldn't readily identify what it was—more anger than fear—more like being provoked than being intimidated. He was so much like someone else in my past—another Big John. That was an awful thing to get in the way of writing a valuable book, but I think from the very first, I knew I couldn't communicate with John. Perhaps Curtis could. Instead, I settled back to study the others on the circus and write about them.

Big John might be the master ringmaster, but Red was real circus, too. He had come from Ringling and was so much a tent man that when the show played an indoor date at Phoenix during the winter, Red had graciously begged off. He couldn't work a tent show indoors.

Robert Johnson—redheaded, red-faced, sunburned, dirty pants, work shoes, usually hungry, always tired, always busy. Red was the real tent boss—the man behind the circus. Without him, the whole show wouldn't get off the ground.

Bob Seaton was the magician and illusionist. We became friends immediately. Whereas Red was impersonal and distant, Bob was warm and chatty. He was half Norwegian and half Italian and he loved my spaghetti. He told me he had been a locksmith and electronics technician by trade before joining the circus. Bob was tall, well built, but slender, fair with still a little boy look about him. He practiced handstands continually and seemed as tireless as Red. He looked great in his skin-tight body suit or in the blue velvet ringmaster's coat he wore when assisting Red. I've seen a lot of illusion acts where the girl is placed in the box and it is skewered with blades, but no one does it as dramatically as the Great Seaton. He confessed to me that he really believed he was the reincarnation of Houdini and that he would never stop until he had topped Houdini's record for escape.

When Bob wasn't being the magician or ringmaster, he helped out with the sideshow. Everyone on the show had more than one job. Even Curtis was kept busy taking money for tickets as well as running the office. But without a steady supply of electricity, I had time on my hands. Nothing was worse than everybody being busy and me not having anything to do. No wonder Neena swayed back and forth on her chain. She had to wait for her next entrance. At least she had her little act to do. I thought of joining the elephant. We could sway together.

The dog was restless too. He could only leave the bus on a short chain. People were always asking me, "Does he bite?" Finally I got tired of it and answered, "No—he swallows whole."

All three performances were a sellout. Curtis sat up there in his little office on the end of Neena's van, wearing his most expensive executive's suit and the broadest, most infectious smile. He glowed so, he might have been taken for a latter day Moses, beard and all. For sure, he was hooked on circus like no one ever was before.

Even though the Southern California evening turned out to be bitter cold, a record crowd queued up, money in hand, reaching for tickets, hoisting pretty babies up to the ticket window to receive family tickets. At a glance, it looked as if each family would be spending around thirty or forty dollars. Then I found out about the family special for eight dollars plus a coupon from the local newspaper. Big John kept his prices reasonable. He gave away free children's passes, but no gatecrasher could get by me. I ran interference on the door, catching any phonies or under-the-tent kids, sending them shamefaced back to the ticket window.

It cost the show nine dollars when a father and mother slipped through in the confusion caused but their dozen or so free kids. That was my job, to stop them at the front door. I stood there each night until my feet ached so badly I wanted to drop to the ground. Finally, noticing my discomfort, John ordered a chair brought to me. From then on, I was to have a chair when I was on duty, regardless of how busy we got. But complaining about standing on my feet was only the beginning.

It helped to get things off my chest. I kept a gripe book. It didn't do any good to complain to Curtis. He was still in his euphoria of this newly discovered career with the circus.

The hours were long. I figured that if we were paid by the hour, we worked for about seventy-five cents. That was a far cry from the twenty-five dollars an hour Curtis made as a translator in Houston.

After driving until three or four in the morning, we had to get up to greet the sponsors. Curtis, who was a night person, wouldn't last long at this pace.

It took a special mentality to enjoy the circus. Besides the children, there were the parents who came in droves, sometimes without their kids. But it was part of being a parent for most of them, to take the children to the circus when it came to town—to have an excuse to go with them. Then there was the adult who came alone.

I was walking toward the donikers when a middle-aged man in a yellow windbreaker hailed me over. Donikers are what circus people call the portable latrines furnished for any public event.

"Hey, do you work for this circus?"

I was in a hurry, but I had to be polite to the patrons. "Yes," I said, trying to get past him.

"Well, tell your boss he oughta get sawdust. The dust is so bad in there, I couldn't see."

"Sorry, we don't have any sawdust."

"You could buy some. Only costs about five dollars a sack," he complained. "Tell your boss he better get sawdust."

There were complainers and then there were the appreciative ones. For Ana and her family, the circus was a very important occasion.

I met Ana on the front door when she lined up with her six babies, waiting for the second performance. She was a pale, stringy-haired woman who looked all used up, but behind the wrinkled and leathered skin shone bright eyes filled with fierce determination to care for what she called her six "cups of love."

Rachel and Caroline were Marshallese from the South Pacific islands. Joshua had been a battered child of a thirteen-year-old mother who abandoned him. The fourth child came from an older woman who had too many children already. Like an old hound with not enough milk, she had rooted the last one out of the nest. The fifth baby had been abandoned on the street. Finding Ann's front door standing partly open, someone shoved a tiny parcel wrapped in newspapers in through the open door. The last baby was a seven-month abortion that lived.

It must have taken some sacrifice to bring them all to the circus. Her husband was overseas, working as a missionary doctor on some remote island. She was trying to sell her house so she would have enough money to pay passage to where he was. To add to her burdens, the last baby was retarded. I thought of her many times after that and the joy of all those children while I told them circus stories at the door.

We traveled to a new town every night. Sandy would go ahead of the caravan, posting arrows for us to follow. One night, we were watching for arrows, and suddenly the trail disappeared. We were about three miles on down the road before we gave up and doubled back. Somehow, we had missed an arrow. All the rest of the show turned off into a shopping mall. We had yet to understand how to read the signs.

Sometimes Sandy did strange things with them. One arrow down and two to the left meant a left turn was coming up soon. Four arrows all facing in the same direction meant that was the turn, right then and now. We learned the hard way. Last night, we ended up in a bank. For the last week, we hadn't gotten the arrows right one time. We either overshot the lot or turned in the wrong place.

No one took time to explain arrows to us. It was assumed that if we were with a circus, we must know circus. Here we thought we were being groomed as managers and we couldn't even follow arrows!

Sandy still wasn't speaking to us. We had no way of knowing whether it was that she was bitterly disappointed with us or if it was a personal matter. There was a lot of gossip on the lot. Rumor had it that she was sweet on Bob, the magician. They fought like lovers, always yelling at each other and finding fault.

Word was also out that the show was in big financial trouble. It would take a miracle to get it out of the red.

John was more sullen each time he showed up on the lot. He stumbled around, face downcast, looking old—thinking old. He was the one who publicly denounced old age as only a matter of thinking. But it had caught up with him and now, he had let loose of the reins. He was old, tired and sick. His only consolation was that Red was gaining more self-confidence as circus manager. Red was his protégé, as close to the real thing as he would ever get. I watched Red every night from my position on the door taking tickets. Red ran through his spiel for the oddity show.

Inside the show trailer were grotesque pictures of human oddities. Red's voice carried down the midway, clear and consistent. He wore dark trousers, a white ruffled shirt and a light blue bow tie. The carrot flame of his hair topped him off like a beacon out at sea.

The entire man was as circus as Dan Rice, one of the founding fathers of the American circus, the prototype of Uncle Sam. If Bob believed he was the reincarnated Houdini, perhaps in time Red could be persuaded to believe he was Dan Rice himself.

But another Red walked the midway by day as circus manager. He worried his way through the days, straining, lugging, bending, lifting, pulling, getting the tent up, getting the tent down, worrying lines in his boyish face, getting beet-red with strain, covering the bright gay hair with an old slouch hat—covering the thin wiry body with worn, often torn, dusty old clothes.

Red always had a cup of coffee in his hand or nearby. It was always the same cup, never washed. It became a part of him, just like the forever cigarette dangling out of his mouth. The cigarette was always there unless he ran out, then he was twice as nervous.

But it was circus that Red was really addicted to. On the midway, he was a magnificent performer. In the ring, he took backstage to no one except that incurable ham, John.

Red was, in every aspect, "*the*" circus, and all it stands for—a tradition on wheels—fantasy in gaily painted old trucks, a song of the open road, rolling down the highway in the middle of the night to a faint path of mysterious black arrows.

5

Red led us from one town to another. Names passed so quickly, I seldom knew what town we were playing in, but I remember some of the characters we met along the road. Every town seemed to have one that stood out.

In that one town had been the complaining sawdust man. The next town had a little old lady who stood out front, blowing smoke in my face. She complained that people inside couldn't see the dog act for the dust kicked up.

"Anyone who can't see the dog act can move to where they can," I said.

But like the man who demanded sawdust, she'd rather stand out front, bitching the whole time, and miss the show.

Then there were the sponsors. We had one sponsor who knew everybody in town. He wanted to let all his friends in free. That night, I think I gave away three quarters of the crowd.

Then there was the middle-aged couple who walked up to me smiling like little children. They didn't have tickets and Curtis had already closed down the ticket window.

"If you both swear you're under six and plant a big kiss right here on my cheek," I turned a cheek toward them, "I'll look the other way and you can sneak in."

We woke up to loud shouts and banging on the door. "You gotta move the bus!"

We were always in the way. I kept telling Curtis, "Please ask Red where it's safe to park so we don't get kicked out of bed so early in the morning."

Curtis had already given up on rising at 7 A.M. to greet sponsors. Only once did a sponsor actually show up that early in the morning. It happened on a day when the trucks were late getting in and the sponsor had to sit in the parking lot all by himself until after 10 A.M.

But getting up early in the morning had its rewards. From across the lot, I could hear the tap-tap-tapping of the sledgehammers, as the men would drive the stakes into the often hard ground. There is a rhythm—a cadence of men, muscles and sheer will power. Most of the men were brawny, all except Carlos. He was slight, compared to the others. The sledgehammer swung him, rather than the other way around. But he worked harder than all the others.

The morning crew knew exactly where to lay out the stakes. I suspected Red went over the ground at dawn, lining up ants in some mysterious formation. Then he sprayed yellow or blue paint on top of them. It must have been because sometimes the "ants" were read wrong and stakes were driven where they didn't belong. Then the men blamed the ants.

My morning began by making coffee for Red, before he went out on his battlefield to spray the ants. Sometimes he would forget. Sometimes he assumed I was still asleep. Sometimes I let Shadow out at just the wrong moment. Red wouldn't come near the bus when Shadow was out on his chain.

While Curtis was still asleep, I set up for breakfast, warmed coffee, set out a tray of orange juice glasses and paper coffee cups, arranged the fruit pies and individual boxes of cereal. I made sure I had enough juice made up and plenty of milk. Sometimes I prepared in advance the ingredients that went into my Elephant Omelettes. I had found a winner with them. Jay Evans, the cowboy trick rider and rope artist, loved combinations of onions, bell pepper, mushrooms, cheese, ham and eggs. Once the others got downwind of Jay's omelette, I had other steady customers like blond, soft-spoken Daryl, one of the candy butchers, and little Cliff who didn't stay with the show very long. I sure missed him when he left. He ate his way through the day. He loved my food so much he brought me gifts. Once it was a flagon of gold he had panned. Another time it was animal stamps for me to use as "outpasses" on the door. I stamped the children's hands with an elephant mark if they left the tent to go to the donikers.

Of course, Curtis was my priority customer, but he always waited for his own breakfast until I fed the workers. Early in the morning when he first woke up, he was hungry for something else. We had it timed to the minute. The men would come for their morning break after they got the sidepoles up in place. By studying their routine, we devised a warning system. First, they laid the canvas on the ground. Then they went around tying each rope to its stake loosely. It was when they began to go around again to hoist the short poles in place that we got our five-minute warning. I got up, quickly dressed and met them at the door all rosy-cheeked and bright-eyed, to serve them breakfast.

Curtis usually stayed in bed and I drew a curtain across the rear of the bus. I'd tend to him later.

On warm days, Ron, the elephant trainer, and Tom, one of the candy butchers, would appear in shorts. Daryl and Carlos worked bare to the waist. Marian wore red tights, white boxer shorts with gay suspenders, white-face and a ringmaster's hat. She didn't come for breakfast but passed by the bus on her way to the shopping mall downtown where she would give out free balloons shaped like tiny tigers and free passes to the afternoon performance. Those free passes—last minute attractions to the show, were designed to attract whole families with each free kid. They were called Day-of-Show tickets.

Often Pie Car morning break would get strung out for hours and Curtis would fall back to sleep. Bob, the magician, always came late. It was one of his jobs to go into town early and arrange for any publicity on the radio stations. He also worked Day-of-Show with Marian.

Another latecomer was little four-year-old Billy. He was the tiny blond son of Peewee and Carmen who ran the concession wagon. Billy was a great conversationalist. He interrogated me about everything. He wanted to "read" my clown picture book. When he had looked at all the clown pictures for the umpteenth time, he began on food cans. He couldn't read, but he knew the difference between Campbell's Cream of Mushroom soup and a can of Van Camp's pork and beans.

Sometimes Billy dawdled over his breakfast just for the sake of dawdling.

I gave him his first lesson in egg peeling. I showed him how to not only peel off the shell but the membrane also. If the egg was shiny, the membrane came off with the shell, but if the membrane remained on the white, it tore and pieces of the white were wasted.

Billy always had a prop with him. Early in the morning, it usually was his own sledgehammer—a pint-sized mallet his father had made for him. Billy swung on the tent stakes with all the ferocity of a full-grown man. The stakes weren't driven too far into the ground, but Billy always managed to draw a crowd.

His knowledge of circus was awesome for one so young. When Billy wasn't driving stakes, assisting Marian, or giving drivers orders, he was riding his Hot Wheels around the midway.

One day, one of the old sponsors who was taking tickets with me at the gate asked Billy if he was going to take his Hot Wheels to Indianapolis some day. Billy stopped v-vrooming and looked up at me, bewildered. In all seriousness, he said in a small clear voice, "Why, do we play there?"

There was one other time in the day when I had a run on the Pie Car—just when I didn't want any business. That was after 5 P.M., just before the first show. The men had gotten in the habit of showing up at the last possible minute before showtime, hungry and usually wanting a big fat ham and cheese sandwich. I could never tell how many might be ordered so I couldn't prepare them in advance. I would quickly drag out ham, cheese, bread and mayonnaise and make two or three sandwiches. Then put it all back in the refrigerator so I could get into my costume and put on my makeup. With one eyebrow to go and still half-dressed, invariably I would hear another knock on the bus door. Out would come the vittles again and I would make another round of sandwiches with a worried eye on the clock.

If I didn't leave the bus by 5:35 P.M., I would be late opening the gate. If Curtis took his sweet time getting out, I had more troubles. He absolutely had to be out of the bus by 5:10 P.M., headed for his ticket window in the back of Neena's van. I needed every minute between 5:10 and 5:35 for myself. All it took was for one of my steadies to insist on soup with sandwich at 5:30.

Getting to the gate on time was one problem. Working it was often another. Sponsors were sometimes more of a worry than customers. Sometimes they were senile and hard of hearing.

One night, five tough Pachucos showed up at the front door of the tent. Their leader, dressed in a white sweatshirt with red sleeves, sneaked under the tent. I saw him because of that unusual shirt, but I couldn't leave my station on the door to chase after him. The next thing I knew, he came back through the gate and the old man assisting me stamped his hand.

"He didn't pay," I said, objecting. The sponsor stared at me blankly.

The Pachuco grabbed his buddy and as soon as I got busy again taking tickets, passed by the old man, waving his stamped hand under the old man's nose. The friend imitated him, waving his hand also. Confused, the sponsor let them both in.

Again, I told him, "They didn't pay."

The next time the Pachucos came out of the tent, heading for a third buddy, I nailed them.

"I saw you sneak in," I said as tough as I could muster. "Now get the hell outta here!" They scrambled.

But a rowdy group of smaller boys didn't scare so easily. They worked like professional hecklers. First, they knocked down the aisle rails. Then they ran behind the concession wagon and busted up the cone trays waiting for refills. They ran screaming like banshees into the sideshow trailer. I ran after them.

It was here I made my first big mistake. I yelled at Curtis as I passed the ticket window, "We got a Rube!" He remembered the old circus distress signal that meant a fight, and came flying out of his cubicle. Approaching the sideshow trailer, he went in one door and I went in the other. The kids tumbled out and spread in every direction—me running after them, yelling at the top of my voice.

I didn't know that "Hey Rube" yelled on the midway was something akin to the red phone that sits on the President's desk—only to be used in case of extreme emergency.

Later, however, that particular bunch of rowdies made peace with the concessionaires. The last I saw of them, they were subdued for the moment and picking up litter on the midway. Peewee would pay them in leftover stale cotton candy at the end of the day.

Pachucos and rowdy gangs weren't as menacing as spaced-out towners. One walked up to me at the front door, asking to see the show. He said he had been hired at $4 an hour for teardown. He wandered back and forth, talking to himself and making weird, disjointed gestures in the air like an animated scarecrow. He seemed particularly agitated at Neena, the elephant. Neena chewed her hay and swayed her ponderous body like a metronome, but all she was concerned about was that he was sober. Neena didn't like drunks. This one was just screwy.

But the female sponsor was more than alarmed. From where she sat in the office beside Curtis, she had a clear view of the "space case's" antics. She complained to Curtis who, in turn, took the matter to Red. Red admitted he had hired the man so that was that.

Later that night, I watched the spaced-out towner work. He was a sight to see. He picked up Billy-sized loads. Spotting some item as far away from the truck as he could see, he walked briskly toward it. He minced along with little Charlie Chaplin steps, moving fast but not covering much ground. He would return, delicately carrying one lone tent spike as if it had a large elephant perched on top of it.

A few nights later, as we crossed over a steep pass from Twenty-Nine Palms to Hemet, I fought to keep awake as I sat behind Curtis. We were always the last ones out. Not only did I have to stay behind until the last worker on the show was fed, but we usually brought up the rear because we were so slow.

"Be careful going downhill," I fussed. "We can't let our brakes overheat." I knew Curtis would get us down safely, but I just had to nag, if for no other reason than to keep myself awake.

"Don't worry," he said, as he put his hand over the gearshift. "I'm going to take this one in granny gear."

"We'll be all night!"

"This is really a bad grade."

I braced myself against the back of his seat and pulled my coat up around my neck. I had my gown on with my robe over it. I had thrown my coat on over my nightclothes to keep warm, but I wanted nothing to slow me down from jumping in bed just as soon as I could. I had settled down comfortably when I looked up ahead in the dark night.

"Look out!" I screamed. "There's an accident up ahead!"

Down below us on the steepest part of the grade, I could see a rig turned over. From the position of the vehicle run up the side of the steep embankment and the camper spilled across the road, it looked like someone might be hurt. Instant adrenalin rushed through my body. It was then that I saw the trailer turned over on its side.

"It couldn't be one of ours, could it?" I said, fearing the worst. "They must be all the way down the road by now. We're so slow."

But they weren't all the way down the road. Marian, Bob and Carlos had stopped at the Seven-Eleven. I had sold Carlos one beer, but he wanted more. When Carlos and Marian came out of the store, Bob told me later that he had decided to sack out in the sideshow trailer.

Back in the trailer that had been altered for the oddities display, Bob had lain down on the bunk behind the false front that was covered with pictures of grotesquely deformed people. There was the famous mule-faced woman and Frank Lentini, the three-legged man. There were pictures of others with huge growths protruding from misshapen bodies.

Bob Seaton, dark-haired, sexy eyed, perfect in body, had been before the public for years. A seasoned circus performer, he twisted and turned in the air high above the ring and struggled to free himself from the strait jacket while being suspended by his ankles. It was a great act. In his second routine, he would prance around the ring with graceful ballet movements, arching his back like Jose Greco, sticking his firm, well-shaped buttocks out and flamboyantly gesturing as he drove swords through Tina in a box.

Bob yawned and stretched out on the narrow bed. He placed his feet firmly against the wall. It wasn't all that easy to sleep with the trailer tossing and rocking down the road, but he was very tired. It had been a long day and a difficult teardown. He worried about the sway. They had tried to get a sway bar attached, but hadn't yet got to a town big enough to find one. He hoped Carlos would take it easy going down the steep grade.

Just two months before, Bob remembered he had turned over in another pickup with a camper. Sandy had been with him. They had both gotten bruised and they totaled the camper. Now he wanted to sleep through it all. Maybe the thought of dumping would go away like a bad dream.

Another reason he wanted out of the camper was that Marian was trying to make out with Carlos. Carlos was just tipsy enough from the beer not to care. But soon Bob was sorry he had committed himself to the trailer as it began to sway wildly. At least up front, he could have seen what was going on up ahead.

He wanted to yell at Carlos to slow down, but no one could hear him in the cab. Then the awful thought struck him—what if Carlos couldn't slow down?! The brakes weren't all that good on the truck. One more thing they hadn't had time to fix.

Later, Bob recalled every minute detail of the accident. He told me, "Before I could determine whether Carlos had really lost the brakes, I felt the sway turn to a roll and I knew I was going over. I braced myself against the wall with my feet and I rolled with the trailer. When it came to rest on its side, I was right side up and standing on my feet. I saw sparks fly past the window. That's when I got the hell outta there!"

"Were you hurt at all?"

"No, just shook up. Then I crawled through the shattered glass and climbed out."

The sideshow trailer had turned over twice. It had broken free of the ball and the safety chain had come loose. When it stopped rolling, it came to rest on its side. Unfortunately, it was on the facade side that Ray Brashears had so carefully painted back at winter quarters. He would be broken-hearted to see the skinned-up golden angels, their wings broken, the gold lettering scraped away and the ornamental top that arched gracefully along the rim of the roof torn off and lying beside the road.

Inside, the displays were all smashed and torn. The heavy refrigerator had tumbled from its niche and had fallen against Bob's suitcases, crushing them. Fortunately, his magic act props were in the office van.

The pickup had spun around and its rear wheel had buried deep in the loose, wind-driven sand. Carlos had just sat in the cab, still behind the wheel, and in shock, but none of them were injured or bleeding.

The first thought that ran through my head was—had anyone been hurt?

My heart pounded furiously as I ran back toward the wreck in my bedroom slippers and robe. Marian met me half way.

"Get back on the road!" she ordered. I had the feeling she wanted to bar me from the accident. "Red has no way of knowing what happened to us if you don't get going!"

Marian sounded calm—too calm. I would have been shaking to pieces if I had just spilled all over the road. Now I felt more apprehension than ever. What if Bob or Carlos were seriously hurt—or even dead? I pushed forward.

"No! You have to catch up with the circus! I'm telling you—the boys are all right, just shaken up. Get to a phone. Have Curtis call John. Tell him—"

Marian's beautiful gray eyes narrowed and her lips set in a determined line, "—tell John that I was driving."

"But Marian, I know Carlos was driving. I saw him pull out."

"You heard me!" she ordered gruffly.

I was confused. I wanted to see Carlos and Bob. I wanted to know that they were all right before we pulled away. In an instant, I pictured Bob lying in the wreck, bleeding. Till that moment, I hadn't realized how close we had become. It was Bob who ran interference for the whole circus with me.

Sometimes I thought Big John had delegated him officially as liaison officer in charge of the cantankerous Cookie!

But I felt fear and uncertainty now. Somehow I obeyed Marian. Her command was too emphatic—like a military order. She was right. Red had to be informed.

I walked back to the bus and gave Curtis the instructions, but we were doubly cautious as we pulled away. In the mirror, I could see that someone else had stopped. They would call the police and a tow truck. Marian would see to that.

6.

It was nearly five A.M. when we finally pulled in behind the circus caravan. Red had sacked out in the cab of the diesel. Sandy woke up when she heard us pull in and joined us in our bus. She wanted to know all the details.

"Poor Bob," she said. "That's the second time—almost the same place too. I mean, that's where we dumped."

So it had been Bob who was with Sandy the night her van rolled while we were still in Houston. I didn't blame the girls for crawling all over Bob. He was as tempting as a piece of forbidden chocolate cake on a diet. Good thing I didn't like chocolate cake.

I thought it was important, finding out that Bob was with Sandy. She'd said over the phone in December, "Me and my boyfriend rolled over in the van."

I don't know why she'd been so cold ever since we left winter quarters. Maybe it was over Bob. It was a stupid thing, but maybe she was jealous because Bob hung around Pie Car so much. Or maybe just financial worries and her trouble with her own family.

One thing good about all that had just happened—we were getting our circus family together. At least we were talking.

I fixed cocoa for all three of us, and Sandy and I sat there visiting, barefoot and shivering. I sneezed. It must have been below freezing in the bus.

"Hey, Sandy," I said, "what happened to the arrows? We lost them. Finally we pulled in an all night grocery and the clerk said we were the fifth vehicle to stop and ask. He sure knew there was a circus in town."

She hum-hawed around. Finally she said, "Couldn't finish arrows 'cause...I got thrown in jail."

Sandy was actually pouting. Then we all laughed. "Sandy—you?"

"It was old warrants. They nailed me here last year doing sound car without permits. I paid the tickets but it was something about having to appear in court. Now I can't run Sound Car tomorrow in this stinkin' town!"

There we were, sitting in the bus at dawn, Sandy in her pajamas and bare-foot—all of us half frozen, three of our people back down the line with a smashed side show trailer and the demolished pickup camper and—Sandy telling us how she got thrown in jail.

"What's worse, Carmen was the only one who had enough money to bail me out!"

When I awoke later in the morning, Curtis said, "Stay in bed. I had a sore throat and high fever. I laced up with gin and orange juice. As soon as Curtis was out of sight, I got up, dressed and headed for the front door of the circus tent. Red came over toward me.

"The sponsors didn't show up," he said. "I'll help you take tickets."

I shook my head. "At least I've learned how to take tickets well." I sneezed.

I felt miserable but I stayed at my station until finally a jolly jaycee with a fat belly and a zipper threatening to pop open showed up and did a fair job of assisting with a stamping of hands.

I was beginning to feel the gin. As soon as I could, I headed back to the bus for a refill. Two good belts later, I forgot my pains. Then the advance man showed up. I gave him a beer and he gave me a squeeze. In fact, he lifted me clear off the ground, squeezed me until something popped, then slid me down the front of him, nice and sexy. I didn't feel a thing for all his efforts except a sharp pain in my back. Flirting with what's-his-name was nothing like going past the ticket window, knowing Curtis was undressing me with his eyes as I walked down the midway. The advance man's advances were nothing like the reality of Curtis.

Somehow I got through the evening, slept a full night's sleep, took lots of Vitamin C and hoped I could revive enough to do the next night's show. I had to get well quick. The show wouldn't wait for me. I would get left behind, like an old Eskimo on an ice floe.

The night was bitter cold, but the next morning was warm and sweet. I was still congested and hoarse, but the sunshine felt good as I stood watching the stake truck unrolling the canvas off its giant spool.

A handful of children turned out for Tent-up. With them was one of the town ladies in a green jogging suit and a funny straw hat slouched down over one eye.

"Greenie" talked with everyone. Her animated hands flew in fanciful gestures as she collared almost everyone on the show. Even from a distance, I could understand almost every word she was saying. Her body moved expressively with her dialogue. Then she finally made her way around to Pie Car and asked for a cup of coffee.

"How much is it?" She rummaged through her cloth purse, but didn't seem to find any coins.

"I have just enough for my men," I said. "Besides, I can't sell to the public. This is a show car."

"Please," she begged. "It's a long way home and I don't want to leave the circus."

She said it like she meant to add—forever. I wanted to be friendly, but if she was some sort of a local authority, I could get shut down by the Board of Health.

She went away, but in a few minutes wandered back again. This time I sat down on the lawn with her to visit. She had a little girl with her who looked very much like Greenie.

She gestured toward the girl. "My granddaughter. I'm raising her—just the two of us. Her parents—I don't know where they are."

I liked Greenie. She was childlike and uncomplicated. I thought at first she might be one of the school teachers but she turned out to be just another grandmother bringing her grandchild to the circus. I had a special feeling for people who never grew up. I was one myself.

Suddenly, I thought of my own grandchildren—of Scotty who was ten now and little Jennie whom I had seen only once. I envied Greenie, having her granddaughter all to herself. Mine would grow up, not knowing anything at all about their own grandmother. I couldn't bring myself to tell my own family I was traveling with a circus. It wasn't that I was ashamed. It was just that I knew they wouldn't understand. I really didn't myself. What was I doing with a raggle-taggle backroad mud show when there wasn't anything I could do on the show?

"You don't think I might help out, do you?" Greenie said. Now here was a real towner. Towners always wanted to help, but seldom knew what they were doing. I knew. I was one.

"I don't know. What can you do?" I said, trying to sound like someone of some authority.

"Oh nothing acrobatic, you know, but I could help with the concessions."
I remembered a group of nuns that worked another show. They ran the concessions and served as wardrobe mistresses. Being a nun or a towner. or an aging circus buff, or even a funny little grandmother in green clothes didn't necessarily exclude one from joining a circus. It was a way of life, not an occupation; a culture, not a company. It was a high honor for it to be said of one, "You're circus." Back there in Willits three years ago when I first discussed going with the circus, Sandy had said that of me. "Terry," she said, "you're real circus." I didn't understand then what it meant.

Now as I sat there talking with a woman who was very much like me—full of dreams, young at heart, adventurous, restless—frightened of dying before she found out what was just beyond the next hill. I knew—it would take grit.
I had to say to her, "We have a full crew now."

She turned away, disappointed. "Well, you know, I really couldn't just up and leave with the circus. I don't have a trailer or a camper. There's my home and all my things, and besides—I have a grandchild to raise."

I couldn't have just upped and left either, but I did. I didn't have a camper or the money to buy one, but I found an old school bus and turned it into a rolling palace, and besides—I had a hungry Doberman Pinscher to care for.

I looked at Greenie's unaged face—no lines, no wrinkles—just a few gray hairs. She wanted so very much to do just what I had done. I wanted to cry out to her, Greenie! Do it now! Do it before it's too late—before you're too old and sick—before you are too discouraged! Life's too short, and even if it was only one season with the circus, or even a few months, it would salt adventure into her heart for the rest of her life!

I watched Greenie walk away slowly, her back to the canvas. The child held her hand, but Greenie paused to look back over her shoulder. The wind picked up its windsong as it flayed the canvas flaps and drummed the centerpole flags. Neena swayed gently back and forth, munching hay. Children began queuing up in anticipation of a few hours magic and total escape from the awesome burdens of life.

I thought of Red, driving himself beyond endurance, Big John working himself when he was too sick to stand up, just so every child in America could see the last of the real old traveling tent shows. It would be sad to grow up never having seen a circus; it would be sadder to want to join a circus with your whole heart and soul being tugged by it and not be able to answer that clarion call of the Pied Piper.

It took a long time to get back over the mountain. Bill Burger showed up again at the next town. He had been the office manager with the show last year. It was his job we had expected Curtis to take over.

Bill Burger was looking for Red, but Red was nowhere to be found. Bob had taken his place early in the morning laying out the grounds for Tent-up. It was unlike Red to miss Tent-up. No matter how wild and wooly a night might be for circus people, everyone had to muster to Tent-up.

I didn't know Bill Burger. I guess he had been popular. Before he left, he made the rounds shaking hands with all the performers. He seemed to know everyone and they all liked him. I was full of envy. I didn't think they would ever like me that way.

Red didn't show up all day, but he was on the midway for the night's show. He didn't look ill, just tired and more nervous than usual. I felt better from my bout with a cold, but the llama was now sick. In fact, he was worse. When we got to Colton, I watched Tina and Bryan give Llary the llama a penicillin shot. I didn't know much about llamas. Curtis didn't either, even though he had been raised in Peru where there were lots of llamas. But Llary didn't have a Peruvian llama sickness. He had some common American animal disease.

We set up the circus near a fake old Western town that had been made for a tourist attraction. It had several expensive gift shops and a large pizza parlor. That night after the show, we were all sitting around the tables eating pizza and guzzling beer. Everyone from the show seemed to be in their own little reverie. I felt like visiting and by now, I knew everyone in the room. I fed these people all day, but here—in public—they treated us as if we were strangers. I began to feel as if I were invisible and my high spirits diminished. It was getting late. I think ours was the last pizza made for the day. I didn't see Bob around. He was Italian, like me. I wondered if he had been in earlier to get his pizza. Nobody had eaten all day from the Pie Car, that was for sure. The last I saw of Bob he was talking quite privately with Red in low tones. Gudrun had come down from the ranch, or at least that was what I heard, but I hadn't seen her. I don't know why, but the hushed, subdued way everyone was acting, I had the feeling something was up, but we hadn't been included in receiving any information.

As I finished the last bite of pizza, licked a thread of stringy cheese off my finger and picked up the final bit of black olive, I thought about how my life had been up until now. I had always had roots, a home of my own and my six children to raise. We hadn't gotten to travel much or take expensive vacations. Even a night out for pizza was a rare occasion. It took two giant pizzas to fill the bellies of our large family. That was all before I met Curtis. When the children were all grown, their father and I parted company. Then I married Curtis and entered into an altogether different world. With Curtis, I could run away with circuses and eat all the pizza I wanted.

I reminisced back to when—there I was, sitting around my huge swimming pool in Houston, worrying about the end of the world coming before I could get a taste of life, when, just at the right time, a circus came to town. On the back of its big red truck was a sign that said: TONIGHT ONLY. Before I knew it, I was traveling down the road with a bunch of clowns, acrobats and jugglers, an elephant named Neena, a crabby bear and fourteen trick dogs.

Curtis accepted it all with philosophic splendor. "Just think," he said, looking out over the lot. "There's nothing there but an empty field. Tomorrow, a circus is going to grow there."

Colton was an important town for us. It was important for Big John and the circus too. He had put Jamie doing advance. Jamie was a hot-shot pitchman. He could charm spinsters into modeling bikinis. The circus was lagging, business wise. There were so many extra expenses. Llary the llama had to have a vet out again. I don't know what it cost, but that's the first time I ever saw a veterinarian with Hollywood chorus girls for assistants. Llary might kick the bucket, but at least he'd go out with a smile on his face.

When the vet gave Llary his shot, the llama went into shock. Tina and Ron stayed with him after the vet drove away. Tina was crying.

When they rolled the llama over, I heard Tina say, "Let's put him in the canvas like we did the lion last year." Ron stretched out a piece of canvas that was used as a part of the midway sidewall, and together they dragged Llary back to Jay's horse van. I had the feeling that was the last of Llary the llama. Now all we had left was one elephant who walked a plank every night and a bear who couldn't do much of anything except sit in his cage moaning and groaning all day.

The next day, word passed down from winter quarters that Llary had died of constipation. I thought it was awfully clean around where he had grazed. At least we didn't have to worry about Neena. She shit up a mountain.

Soon after, though, the worst thing that could plague a circus happened. We survived wrecking the trailer, losing our llama, the clutch going out on the sleeper bus and the flu hitting half of the circus performers all at once. What was about to hit us now was more disastrous than a blowdown. That was loss of esprit de corps.

We had driven all night to get to Phoenix, the longest hop between stands so far. We all looked forward to the two-day stop like it was a children's Christmas. We needed rest badly, but we got more than we bargained for.

I felt a wave of apprehension when I saw the immaculately manicured lawns, the imposing, castle-like hotel frowning down on our ragged little tent with its myriad multitudinous holes, patched and unpatched, and the sprawling golf course, the miniature artificial lakes, each with three smartly trimmed weeping willows planted in exactly the same configuration.

We pulled in late. The only place left to park was beside Neena's van. She had already peed up a storm. A river of smelly yellow urine dribbled down the side of the van and onto the neat clean black asphalt.

Being downwind of Neena wasn't exactly a choice place to park but we had to have electricity. There were no stationary hookups. We were dependent upon the noisy old generator. There were no public donikers either. I would be bothered all night by people complaining that they had to walk all the way up the hill to the hotel to use the restrooms.

There wasn't even a decent place to stake the animals without having to curry their droppings out of the tightly packed grass.

I looked at us, road-dusty by now, old trucks, older pickups—sad little mud show! In such an elegant setting, I couldn't help but have a Cinderella complex. In all that sprawling spaciousness, we had been allotted only a tight little corner of the grounds used as an overflow parking lot. It was like being horribly dirty cousins from the country whom everyone was ashamed of and tried to hide till the visit was over. However, the hotel graciously offered us their $150 a night rooms at half price!

Everyone was snapping, sullen or silent. No one made any money if there was no crowd. Tom only sold two candy flosses all night.

"I guess when you're a senior citizen," I said, trying to cheer him up, "popcorn and cotton candy stick to your dentures."

What few people showed up must have all been friends of the sponsor. A sponsor is supposed to be like a high-pressure front agent who packs them in. That's because the way Big John operated, most of his shows were booked by charities. The sponsor represents the charity and boosts sales, then takes a cut for the charity. No one in this neck of the woods knew much about charity—or ticket sales.

The sponsor made a huge noise about the tickets not arriving in time, the newspaper publicity being weak and, when he ran out of all that to bitch about, he complained that the tickets were a different color this year. But while he was distracting everyone's attention, he let several groups of well-heeled senior citizens in on family tickets. They all claimed they were related. The family ticket was designed to have a mother and father accompany a whole houseful of small children. The only kid I noticed all night was a well-dressed little girl who was dropped off by a chauffeured limousine.

I had a crowd, if you could call it that, through the gate by 6 P.M. I went back to the bus to rest until the second show.

"It's no use," Red said, absolutely crushed. Nothing hurt him more than for people not to love or appreciate his circus. He would rather have a straw house packed with free passes than to play to a cold house—a group of disinterested spectators.

Back in the bus I watched through opaque drapes the slowed down movement of the circus people. They didn't seem to know what to do with themselves without the tent to take down that night and load up. Finally, I saw Marian's pickup depart with a load of the boys, heading toward the heart of town for a little hell-raising.

I could hear Neena swaying restlessly in her van. Ponies neighed into the wind as a few drops of rain splattered on their backs.

Tina brushed by the bus, but this time not to tend her ponies. She was crying. We heard her yell out to someone following her, "I want to be alone!"

"Do you think I better go after her?" I asked Curtis, but he shook his head no.

"It's not any one thing," he said. "She's reacting and feeling terribly insecure. They all are."

"Do you think that's dangerous?"

"No, but we can stand by, although I don't exactly know what we can do. You know Tina and Sandy have been so close?"

"Yeah." I remembered the first day when Sandy had made a point of introducing Tina as her "best" friend.

"Now there's trouble between them."

"Does Sandy blame Tina for Llary dying?"

"No, but Tina's father came to visit her and he's staying with the circus a few days. It seems that Sandy pulled 'owner's daughter's rank' and said he couldn't hang around. Tina blew up."

"I don't blame her, but then I see Sandy's side, too. We don't exactly have guest accommodations."

"Tina is seriously considering leaving the circus."

"That would be terrible, wouldn't it?" I tried to sound sincere, but down deep I thought how sick I felt every time Curtis got eye-glued on Tina's well-shaped rear end.

I knew trouble was brewing between Tina and her husband, Bryan. He spent more time in the tent than he did in their trailer. Having Daddy around would make it easier for Tina to leave her husband as well as the circus. Daddy meant permanence, security and love.

But Tina was loyal. She was "circus" just like Sandy and Red. Red's whole life was tied up with the circus. Every cent he could make was going to pay back a debt. He was a bundle of nerves, running on the fumes of energy. Half the time he couldn't eat; the other half, he wouldn't. The flame of hair, the white shirt with its ruffles, the oversized tuxedo pants—all gave him the appearance of a lighted candle on a dark night. But an ill wind of bad spirit on the show threatened to extinguish that candle.

In the dark of night, rain splattered noisily on the top of the bus. Outside were sounds of restless animals—Neena thumping the sides of her van, the bear moaning fretfully as he paced endlessly up and down in his bread truck and—faintly above the sounds of the night—Tina crying.

7

It had begun to rain while we were still at the swank hotel, but with the canvas already up and the thick green grass absorbing the run-off, we didn't feel particularly uncomfortable even though it was raining steadily. The first indication we had that it had really been raining hard was after we loaded up and got on the move. We passed swamped street corners and flooded storm gutters and drove through deeper and deeper puddles.

We turned off the freeway onto lowland and muddy fields. The caravan found its lot and one by one we pulled off to bed down for the night.

In the morning, we woke up to find almost every vehicle stuck in sticky, soggy, gluey red brick clay. All the vehicles except one of the pickups sank rim deep into the clay mud. I heard Neena trumpet. I peeked out through the curtains. She had her thick leather harness on and was tugging at the sleeper bus.

Ron goaded her in her tender spot under her arm. She dropped to one knee to get traction, but the heavy bus wouldn't budge. Everyone—workers and performers alike—got behind the sleeper and pushed. Neena trumpeted again, a low sorrowful note of defeat. She was telling them it was no use. This was a three-elephant bog-down.

One by one, like animals following each other in the ring, the other trucks spun their wheels until they were helplessly trapped in the miry clay. If they had put planks down, they might have been able to back up to safety. Instead, they pulled forward into deeper trouble.

From his comfortable motel where he had been spending the night, Big John emerged like a fairy prince to rescue his circus. Instead of appearing in shining armor, or better yet—a Superman suit—he came dressed in a light blue suit that matched his eyes. Somebody handed him two black garbage bags.

Unceremoniously, John stepped into them and tied them on his legs with pieces of rope.

When the promoter, whose name was Don, showed up, all John said was, "Don't talk to me about Arizona."

We would have to "sidewall it"—play without the Big Top—with only the side canvas in place. No way could the reel truck plow its way across that mire to lay down the main tent. Afraid to move the bus for fear we would bog down also, we settled back to watch a soggy show put itself together.

Out the window, we could see men currying ponies covered with muddy water, clowns trying to keep costumes clean, everyone wearing unclownly hip boots, balloons gaudily displaying yellow, red, green, pink against hazy skies—darkening skies—storm-threatening skies.

The sun peeped through and patches cleared away some of the gloom. We could have dried out in the Arizona sun. Mountains rose from the valley floor—purple mountains' majesties against blackening skies beyond. But the intermittent rays of the sun failed to dry us.

There was mud everywhere, except on our precious canvas tent still rolled on its reel. Sidewalls, like portable bathhouses on a public beach, screened around the pay show.

I heard the generator start up, but I had no power. I could see my two extension cords in the mud. They had been unhooked at the generator.

"I don't care whether the bologna spoils or not," I said bitterly to Curtis.

"We aren't important. I can't even get electricity when the generator's on."

"You're feeling better," he said. "I can see."

Poor Curtis! I had told him I would follow him anywhere. Already I was complaining. Jokingly, I said, "Why don't you put pontoons on the bus and we can sail for Australia?" Then I thought too late—that's the kind of left-handed remark that led us to joining the circus in the first place.

"Are you sorry you joined the circus?"

"No, but I hate this—oh, forget it."

Later in the day, I tried to talk to Red about the country club show and what had gone wrong. "Circus is for kids," I said, hoping he would be communicative, "—children sitting in the dust."

I thought, yeah—sticky-fingered kids, sitting in the dust, munching popcorn, dragging grandpas along the midway—riding elephants. Noise, clutter, make-believe—that was circus. But not for prosperous senior citizens who live in $150 a day retirement hotels and drive up in Rolls Royces.

"Yeah," Red said. "Circus is for kids."

It started to rain again. That meant a "John Robinson" show—a cutting short of all the acts. Without the aerial rigging, there wasn't much of a show anyway.

Nor an audience. Only about twenty brave people showed up. I didn't even bother to slosh through the mud. Curtis was handling the tickets by himself.

I could hear Jay's act. He must have gone on seven times. The horses were the only ones who could make it through the mud. By intermission, most of the paying customers had walked out.

John Strong stood by the entrance watching the unsatisfied customers leave. The light blue suit was now covered with mud up to his knees.

I watched Sam the clown staring vacantly at one of the horses pawing and whinnying. He vocalized the bad news that a "mud down" was worse that a blow down. Sam shared his misery. It had been a poor house. No coloring books were sold at all. Marian needed every cent she could get from her concession. She was saving her money. She never ate much, just an occasional sandwich or glass of milk. Sam was circus and both were rained out.

I had been with them long enough to see the heartbreak even when they didn't complain. It was a thankless job, as poorly paying as could be and without much real hope. Only a few would go on to better shows. Circus was more than that. They put their heart and guts into their performances.

I had to remain on the sidelines, just watching. We weren't "circus" enough to be taken into their confidence. I felt bad about the show hurting so—bad stands, lousy weather and now this. But there was little we could do. We had shared the ordeals of the road with them—even this mud and cold. In the past ten days alone, everything had hit us but a blowdown. Yet, they kept moving on—tent up, tent down and on to the next town.

One by one, the trailers pulled out as the ground hardened enough to support the weight of the lighter vehicles. But the office van wouldn't budge. Slowly, the men loaded up the dogs, goats and ponies. Last of all, Ron goaded Neena in and shut the door.

Ron pulled backward with the already freed reel truck, but nothing happened. In a little while, a farm tractor was requisitioned. The little tractor reared straight up in the air, then spun tread in the soft clay.

Men pushed frantically like panicked bees, not sure whether they were working for or against their own efforts. The beautiful big red and blue van stayed stuck in the mud. Then the tractor was moved around to the rear where, with wheels on drier land, it could get better traction. All the men got behind and pushed.

The tractor huffed and puffed and pulled. Neena trumpeted a complaint from within the van against the jostling. But the big semi with huge lettering across its side that said CIRCUS remained imprisoned.

Big John had disappeared for several minutes. Then, from clear across the field I heard him holler, "The only way to get out of here is to throw 2x8s under the wheels after digging them out!"

I turned to Curtis, "Why didn't they do that sooner?"

"I guess nobody thought of it."

"Why don't they at least take the elephant out?"

"Nobody thought of it."

We had watched while the men had loaded all the heavy props into the van. Then they loaded all the animals in, and two-ton Neena last. With all that aboard, they had tried to push the overloaded van out of the mud.

We continued watching as they put hay and wire under the wheels until they got enough traction to break free of the clay and back out.

Daryl came across the street to where we were now parked and bought a soda pop.

"I see the truck's free. How come it's not running?" I asked.

"They broke the fuel tank getting the truck free."

I turned to Curtis. "That does it, then. We might as well pull out. No sense of us hanging around here any longer. They might be here all night."

"Do you want me to drive for you tonight?" Daryl asked.

"No, that's all right," I said, staring at his grimy clothes covered with wet clay up to his waist. "If we get tired, we'll just pull over and rest."

As Curtis warmed the motor, I saw I still had my sign up in the window which had been placed there earlier in the day. It said:

MUD PIE CAR. OPEN AS USUAL.

We hadn't gotten very far down the road when I asked Curtis to pull off the freeway into Phoenix for supplies. We stalled at the first light.

"Oh no! Not the starter again!" I wailed as Curtis calmly removed it and tried to repair it by candlelight. This time it failed to respond. Finally, Curtis stuck the starter in a sack and hailed a ride into town.

It was very quiet out there on that spur road, that is, until after Curtis had left. Suddenly the sound of an airplane was deafening. I looked out the window.

We had broken down on the edge of an airport runway. A few feet from the bus was a huge sign saying:

DANGER. LOW-FLYING AIRCRAFT

The next plane that flew overhead, I ducked. At least we weren't parked on a railroad track this time.

Curtis took forever coming back. I had lots of time to think. I worried about Neena, and I also worried about the dogs in their cages hung on the wall of Neena's van. I worried about Sandy's hand. She had stabbed herself with her own saber while doing one of her acts. I had cleaned it out and bandaged it as best I could, but she needed it tended to professionally. Would she remember to soak it in salt water like I said? And Red. He was so tired. He hadn't eaten all day. Neither had the other men, but once they were on the road, they would probably stop somewhere.

I returned to worrying about Neena. She seemed to be more restless each day. I had noticed the panel kicked loose on her van. Without our elephant, there was no show. Then I came up with something to really worry about. We still had the cash boxes. How could they open up tomorrow without the cash boxes?

I began to fantasize.

We were near an airport. Maybe we could rent a plane, fly over the circus and drop the cash boxes to them. Then I could see the boxes bursting open and all the cash blowing out. No, that wouldn't work. I came up with another idea. I could hire a bush pilot to fly real low. I could—no, I couldn't. I was afraid of heights. What would I wear? What if the chute didn't open? I could see the headlines in the local newspaper:

COOKIE FLIES TO THE AID OF HER CIRCUS.
Retired grandma who ran away with the
circus saves day by flying over circus in old
crop duster to deliver the missing gate money.

Then I thought, *I'll probably be upstaged by that uncurable ham, John, rescuing us in the middle of the night with a tow truck.*

But he didn't. Curtis called Gudrun in Yucaipa and she gave him John's hotel room number. Curtis called and called, knowing the van with the ruptured fuel tank was somewhere back there being repaired. If Red could only be contacted, we could still be rescued. Curtis called Gudrun back and left a message in case John called. We settled down to wait.

Sunday morning came, the air traffic diminished and we slept in. There was no place to get a starter for a '57 Chevy school bus on a Sunday morning. We would have to wait until Monday morning to find an auto electric shop. We had missed our first show. Would we ever be forgiven?

The starter was repaired before noon on Monday and we were on our way again. We had a long road to cover between us and our circus. They played Lake Havescu without us. I wondered if Bob tried to jump off the London Bridge? He said he would try if they'd let him jump handcuffed and in his straitjacket just like Houdini would have done.

I thought of the circus as we drove down the beautiful Arizona highway. At least the circus was responsible for us seeing some lovely scenery. The road rolled through flat land, small towns, past whistlestops, truck stops and wayside stores. The desert land in late winter was a blaze of orange-flowered glory. There were purple lupines between huge rocks, sage and scrub and Joshua trees blooming in pre-springtime splendor.

Beyond a thousand shades of green, the purple mountains rose straight up from the valley floor. Blues and grays and purples—shadowy specters farther away than they seemed.

We passed San Domingo Wash where the road cut through red rock mountain. In moments, we were in a different terrain.

The road had once been a trail settlers took on their way to California. Some stopped to form communities with names like Surprise, Arizona. Others gathered rocks from nearby mountains, built sturdy houses and eked out a living until civilization caught up with them. Now, their descendents made a living selling roadside antiques and cold beer.

We passed Mockingbird Hill, Scat Hill, the Ol' Fishing Bar and dropped down into Wickenburg. We crossed the swollen angry Hassayampa River almost at flood stage. However, the quiet little town with its curved streets and old red schoolhouse showed no signs of panicking with the river so high. Curtis called this Zane Gray country. I asked him why.

"When I was a little boy, I used to read a lot of Zane Gray books. My favorite was one called *Desert Gold*. It was written about this part of the country."

We had driven a long time and now we were in high desert where the main growth was manzanita and scrub oak. The large fluffy plants that bloomed alongside the road were ones that later would dry to become tumbleweeds. The sharp, daggered mountains seemed closer, their ridges were like scales on the back of some pre-historic monster sleeping—daring not to be awakened.

I was tired and sleepy too. I tried to write as the bus bounced down the road, but all I got for my efforts was a pageful of squiggles.

I looked at my watch. It was already 1:30 pm and we still had another ten miles to go. The show had traveled this part of the desert by night. What a shame! In a way, I was glad we had broken down when we did, so we could see the desert by daylight. In another week, the Joshua trees might not still be in bloom. Huge yellow-green starbursts on the ends of the branches brought incredible beauty to the funny green monster cacti. Those Joshua trees, when not in bloom, stood silent desert scarecrows with oddly contorted limbs askew.

We passed swollen washes turned into muddy rivers. In this country, at this time of year, whole roads could disappear in one night from sudden downpours and flash floods.

I don't know how we did it in the old bus, but we made it just in time for the first show. As we rounded the last corner, Curtis was hurriedly dressing while still driving. I fed first one arm and then the other into his sleeves. He had gotten his longjohns on backward and his shirt buttoned wrong, but he grabbed the cash boxes and made it to the window just in time to open.

Surprisingly, Tom, the candy butcher, was the only one to scold us. "You should have told the cops and they would have told Red. Then we could have had our starting money."

I wanted to tell him that we spent all night in the middle of a freeway, and for once, the cops didn't stop and hassle us, but he hurried off.

It was a good thing to know we were missed. But then, we had the cash boxes.

Soon the tent was down again and we were heading for Bullhead City. If we had been in granny gear for most of the trip so far, we never appreciated those low gears as much as now.

We descended steeply to the Mojave Desert floor. I mean, like straight down—a trucker's nightmare!

We smelled of burnt rubber by the time we finally reached bottom and Bullhead City on the cold clear Colorado River. I wasn't too sure just where Bullhead City was. I had never heard of it before, but one thing was obvious—the other side of the road was in Nevada. Rows of gaudily lit casinos lined the north side, making the desert, even in the quiet of winter, bloom like a neon rose.

8

The next morning, I awoke to welcome warm sunshine. I dressed and joined some townspeople sprawled on the lawn. The children called out to Neena by name.

"How come they know the elephant's name?" I asked.

"Last year, this same circus came through here in June. It was so hot they led her down to the river to cool off. Once they got her in, they couldn't get her out."

"I wonder if she remembers it," I said, as I looked around for my elephant. Neena was leisurely sunning herself on the far edge of the lawn.

I was more concerned with the Fire Marshall. He hovered nearby with a scowl on his face. Later in the day, when the crowd began pouring in, he was still scowling. I made an extra trip through the tent to nail any smokers. I tried to keep the aisles clear and the crowd controlled but this was one of those nights we called a "straw house," where kids were plastered in the straw, or grass as it was here, all the way to the ring curbs.

The show was always supposed to start by 6 pm. At 6:30, kids were still lined up to ride Neena. Here, as never before, she was the supreme star of the show. Everyone in town wanted to ride Neena. After the incident last June, this whole town considered her their own personal elephant.

Finally, I had to call time on Red. I knew he wanted to squeeze the elephant rides for all he could, but those "pachydermophiles" would rather ride an elephant all night than see a circus on time.

Red looked up at me with those incredibly blue eyes, rosy little boy cheeks and flaming hair. He was a rainbow in a baggy tuxedo. He was an elf in a Master of Ceremony's top hat. He was flustered, maybe even put out at me for being bossy, but I was hearing Gudrun's command, "Open on time."

What would Big John have said? Of course he would say, "Let them ride Neena all night if they want to."

A few minutes later, Red called time on Neena's rides. She wasn't needed until the last act. Till then, she would restlessly sway to and fro on her chain with that graceful elephant ballet of hers.

Candy butchers drifted by the bus for snacks. I was half-napping when one of them yelled, "Did you hear? Neena got loose!"

"How?" I said. I had seen men fixing her van earlier, patching the holes with heavy angle iron.

"She pulled her stake and just walked off. First thing, people down by the river complained she was peeping in their camper windows. Old ladies came flying out screaming."

"Was she going down to the river?"

"She sure was headed that way."

"That figured," I said smiling. Neena had remembered.

Neena looked like she was still thinking about the river as Ron hosed her down the next day in the next town. Across the street from where the tent was set up, I heard two men shouting at each other.

"Hey, Harry! Did you know there's an elephant taking a bath in our back yard?"

Neena grunted, lay down and rolled over.

"Yeah, he's with the circus."

"Is that your elephant?" Harry yelled at Ron, who was scrubbing Neena's back with a wire brush.

"Yes. Thanks for the water."

"How often do you bathe it?"

"Every day," Ron said, smiling. He was a very dark black man and when he smiled, his teeth flashed like a commercial.

"Golly," the man said. "Must be the cleanest or the dirtiest elephant around. My wife doesn't even bathe that often."

The men went back to their work, accepting their large guest graciously. I walked over toward Ron and Neena.

"I hear she took off yesterday."

"All she did was look in some windows," Ron said defensively, like an over-protective parent.

I looked at Neena's face. I could swear she winked. I wonder what she saw in those camper windows.

Ron spoke a soft command and Neena rolled over on her side. Ron sat down on her to rest.

"Do you command her in Senghalese?"

"What's that?"

"The dialect of the province where she most likely was born." I said it like I knew what I was talking about.

"Oh, I know she's an Asian elephant, if that's what you mean," he said, unimpressed. "But I never heard of Senghalese."

"That's the language usually spoken to elephants." Snootily I added, "The commands are <u>hedda</u>—lie down, <u>dit</u>—back, <u>delah</u>—come here, <u>belah</u>—foot up and <u>brruh</u>—push. I thought I heard you say something like that."

"Nope," he scowled. "I just talk plain old street talk to her."

There I was, doing it again—embarrassing myself, shooting off my mouth—trying to sound important, like I really knew something about the circus.

But I wasn't the only big bag of wind. All day long the canvas billowed like a fat man with his cheeks full of marshmallows. The side canvas blew freely like an Irish woman's laundry. We were high on a hill. If the canvas took off from that height, we'd be chasing it halfway to Arizona.

Maybe we were going to have a blowdown. After all, it had happened in Oregon, a few years back. Now, once again, Big John Strong's canvas tent was facing high winds, black skies and approaching rain. How bad would things get before we had to cancel a show?

In Hesperia, it finally happened. Red had to call a "John Robinson" on the first show. Big John himself cancelled the second. It was bitter cold and had begun to snow. By 8 P.M., the men had the tent down. Peewee and Cliff were pulling poles down while the crowd was still watching the show.

Jim, the juggler, tried to get some of the blow-off crowd—those leaving the main tent—into the side show to see Oz and his wonder dog, which really was Curtis Cainan and his raggedy little dog, Suzie. "You'll wonder what she's going to do next, folks," Jim bellowed, but no one cared.

I knew what I was going to do—feed those guys and get the hell out of this California North Pole!

Even before showtime, the men huddled in my warm bus, drinking coffee and discussing how to pull the switch on the second show. "Old Blue Eyes" Red sipped his steaming coffee and puzzled for a moment before breaking into his familiar Master of Ceremonies routine.

"Ladies and Gentlemen, now we have the greatest show of all. Seaton, the man of mystery, will perform the impossible feat. He will, before your very eyes, make this entire circus disappear!"

I think they would have all remained in the Pie Car through the rest of the show if the sponsor, a brisk little gray-haired woman, hadn't come banging on the door.

"Is Curtis in there?"

"Erickson?" I yelled back.

"Yes."

"No, he's in his office."

"I thought this was his office."

"No, this is his residence." I suppressed a giggle.

"Then who are all those men in there?"

Red stepped to the door, opened it a discreet crack and pointed. "The office is in that red van over there."

She tried her best to peep inside but Red spread himself across the doorway. I looked at the men. A knowing smile spread around the room.

"What's the matter with her?"

"We've been here before," Bob said.

"She does look kind of bossy," I said, "but Curtis can handle her, I'm sure."

Somebody snickered.

"Besides her, did any other sponsors show up to work the door?"

"Oh yeah, they're all over the place."

"Good. I can stay in the bus and keep warm. Some of those sponsors are nothing but trouble. I had one of them argue with me about how big is twelve years old."

"Yeah," Red said. "How do you decide when they stand there and lie to you?"

"If they've got titties, or if their voice is hoarse," I said. "Or if they shave. You gotta watch those teenagers."

"The ones you have to really watch," Red said, pokerfaced, "are the ones who have titties and also shave."

After the men left the warmth of the bus, I heard the African pygmy goats bleating sorrowfully. It had begun to snow. After loading up, we all sacked in and slept the night in the tear-down lot. Big John was afraid to pull the heavy rigs out on the ice-slick roads. Later, we found out that almost everyone gave in to the cold and found motels, which they could little afford. Curtis and I remained in the bus, cozy and warm—arms and legs entwined under two heavy sleeping bags.

9

The next day, when we pulled up to the half-erected tent, an animal control officer was giving Jay a hassle. Lancaster was in Los Angeles County, which meant dozens of extra permits and regulations were required. Red had to go down and fight them all through Lancaster City Hall, then had to run over to Palmdale to take care of final arrangements there. When he came back from Palmdale, he was furious.

"Jamie didn't show up at the newspaper office in time, or do the radio promotion and—" he was turning pink all over, "—there were misprints on the posters!"

I couldn't help but feel sorry for Red. He took everything so seriously. It was true that the show had yet to break even. Curtis was fighting the audit books.

Even I found my Pie Car business was way off. Some days, no one came all day long, unless it was one of the Rivera brothers for coffee before teardown at night.

However, the slack in business allowed me some quiet time. There were those moments during teardown, when I was completely alone. I could get out my notebook and recount the day's events. Sometimes I just sat and stared out the window. Earlier, the air was filled with sound—generator roaring, side show noises, someone hawking the show, music from the big tent announcing each act. But now, all was quiet. Even the generator had been turned off and I sat in darkness for a while, writing.

Candles wallow in buttery pools of tallow. Shadows dance on walls in eerie choreography as day ends. There is still a chill in the air. Snow is packed down on the mountain for the last of the winter skiers.

For three solid weeks we have had adventure, excitement, breakdowns—troubles galore. Since we left Arizona, we have been rained out, nearly blown down at Needles and, last night, the show had to be shortened because of the intense cold.

The next day, however, the weather was in the balmy sixties, the sun was pleasantly warm and the winds were still. The circus was ready to receive a good crowd. Would our luck hold? Were things going to go right for a change?

Just before showtime, Tom noticed a small rip in the canvas. Taking a repair kit with him, he climbed aloft to patch up the far end. The cold had made the canvas brittle. I remember reading how Circus Vargas had lost a whole tent that way. Tom moved cautiously. Then with no warning, the canvas ripped further and Tom fell over ten feet to the ground with a sickening thud. He hadn't really fallen far—the ground was soft turf—but he fell across the seats, injuring his back.

Tom lay motionless.

"Is he conscious?" someone said.

"Yes…just the wind knocked out of him."

"Wiggle your fingers, Tom." Tom wiggled one finger.

"He'll be okay."

But the ambulance was called and Tom was taken to the local hospital. Everyone went back to work, but they were visibly stunned. What would happen next?

There are no more superstitious people than circus folk. Trouble always comes in threes, they say. After what happened to Tom, all the performers were uptight.

That night, we had a "paper" house. That meant almost everyone was in on a free pass. I left my station on the door when I could see absolutely no one else was coming in. I seldom got a chance to see the show because I was always taking tickets. Tonight, I decided to be a spectator.

Chris and Ron were introduced for their perch act. Ron Pace, his handsome black body encased in a silver body suit, walked up a small flight of stairs carrying blonde, long-haired Chris Kennington high in the air on the perch pole. They had done it thousands of times before. Ron balanced the pole on his shoulders while beautiful Chris sat very still, but coming down the other side of the stairs, the perch began to sway. Chris fell clumsily into the "mechanic," the safety wire aerialists wear.

The ground crew quickly rescued her and the audience traditionally applauded. She didn't seem to be hurt, but I ran out crying. What would happen to our little circus next? Now I began looking for trouble—the third trouble. It'd have to be Neena. I looked over to where she was staked. She was leaning way over her border rope, reaching for a patron with her trunk. She had pushed so hard, the rope pole had fallen over. With that barrier rope down, capricious Neena was inviting people to come within her grasp. Remembering that she had just slammed Curtis up against the side of her van that very morning, I yelled out a warning.

"Get back! Get away from that elephant!"

I circled the van and moved the patrons back away from her. Then I hit the corner stake as hard as I could with Peewee's mallet and wound the rope tight.

But Neena was still too close to the rope. That meant only one thing. She had torn up her stake again and was loose! When I saw the chain dangling on one foot, but the other end lying limply along the ground, I ran for help.

Red was announcing the acts in his Master of Ceremonies outfit. Bob stood by to assist him. I hesitated. Red wouldn't like me to interrupt him unless the tent was on fire. Instead, I motioned to Bob to come over to the net.

"I think Neena's loose again," I said in hushed tones.

"Not again," Bob said, slipping under the net. Red gave me a dirty look.

Disregarding my intrusion, he continued without interruption those same words he said night after night.

Bob followed me out of the tent. By the time we got there, Daryl was at Neena's side but the chain wasn't loose. The stake had been driven all the way into the ground so that only the chain was visible and Neena couldn't get a hold of it to pull it up. Why should they inform me? But then they didn't expect me to be that green and stupid.

Ron came to get Neena. I could see he was angry. Red must have told him I disturbed the show. It was time to bring Neena around for the elephant rides anyway. Earlier, she had gotten into the dog food. This last scene wasn't her fault. It was mine. Poor Neena—hanged if she does and hanged if she doesn't. For me, at least, this was the third disaster of the day.

After teardown, the workmen carried the last of the performing gear—the props—to the office van. Chris walked by, back straight, head high, but already the after-show metamorphosis was taking place. The trim thighs, the silky body, the spangled briefs were all concealed beneath baggy drawstring jogging pants. The tiny breasts covered with turquoise Spandex and sparkling gems were now swathed in a dingy sweatshirt. Only the false eyelashes and the glitter stars pasted on her eyelids remained.

Chris—tiny little Chris was my fantasy. When she worked her aerial act, I pretended it was me. For that one moment, I was held spellbound as if I had been scooped up by some unseen hand and placed on that stainless steel perch. I cried when she fell. I was frightened. I had fallen, too.

I watched Neena tethered near our bus. She stopped swaying when Jay or Ron walked by. Then she resumed her restless but graceful rhythmic dance, stopping only to check her stake. Every inch of the chain was securely in place. She ran her silk-smooth trunk back and forth. The chain held fast. The heavy chain ran taut. The stake was buried deep in the ground. She had dropped neat piles of manure all day.

Usually Tina removed it with a large shovel, but the show broke early. Neena maneuvered in a small area to avoid stepping in the excrement. She was such a fastidious two-ton lady. Sometimes I felt as trapped on a chain as she was.

Like Neena, I didn't go very far when I got loose either. Just the same, I often wanted more space than I had—enough to get out of the shitpiles of my life.

Now I had done it to myself again. I had had a run-in with Gudrun, the boss's wife. Neither she nor John were fully aware of everything that went on. I had liked Gudrun from the very beginning. I remember the first time I met her. I was amazed at how young and beautiful she was. After all, John was old. That doesn't sound fair to say it like that, but it was the truth.

Recent ill health, diabetes and being a reformed alcoholic had aged him before his time. One can't booze it up, sugar coat it and burn it at both ends without suffering the consequences. Of course, he had found Gudrun before he began disintegrating so rapidly. John had been quite an outstanding personality in his day—showman, magician, animal trainer, movie star, friend of celebrities, ringmaster and now owner of a well-known Western circus. He had managed to keep his circus running over forty years. But this last year and the problems with the show were hurting him.

Gudrun had come to his aid. She took over a lot of the responsibilities of the show, including the finances. In effect, she was my boss.

Now I had had to sit there in her little compact car, listening to her go on and on in broken English so fractured I could only understand every other word, and all it was that she was fussing about was outdated gossip.

"The men say zat you don't get up and fix zair breakfast," she went on.

That had to be Red complaining. He wouldn't add that he was the only one who ever wanted anything before break time and then, just a cup of coffee.

"And zat you fix them frozen sandwiches."

The other side of that coin was the electricity I had been promised and didn't get. One time we were plugged in all night on a fairground plug. The next morning, unused to such overabundance of refrigeration, I found the bologna frozen. Someone was in a hurry, wouldn't take excuses, so I shrugged, sliced off a rigid bit of meat and said lightheartedly, "Hold it in the sun for a few minutes and it'll be all right."

Goodgawdalmighty! Imagine a circus without a sense of humor!

But nevertheless, that's the three-week-old bitching that finally got back to the head office at winter quarters, and that, belatedly, Gudrun was digging up the dead bones of in her rotten, broken English and thick German accent.

I sat there, taking it until she started complaining about Curtis. "He's arrogant," she said. "And if he doesn't get the hang of the office soon, I'll have to dock his wages."

Now my blood boiled.

"Dammit!" I said. "Neena gets more pay in dog food than we do between us! We were making as much in Houston in one day as you pay us for all week!"

"Now you calm down, Terree," Gudrun said, "you don't need to get zis angry. Zat's your trouble. You don't want advice. You should ask Carmen how to run za Pie Car." She tossed her beautiful head of rich dark hair as if going to Carmen would solve everything.

"Ask Carmen?" I went into a blind rage. "I understand she ran Pie Car last year and everything was so dirty, the men refused to eat. And I'm supposed to learn from her?"

"I was only trying to make suggestions." She forced a cold smile from the corners of her pretty little lips. No wrinkles, no gray hair, but she had a daughter old enough to be in a woman's beauty contest. Gudrun was vivacious, salty and spoiled. She could have fired me on the spot. I'll never understand why she didn't.

"You know what, Gudrun?" I looked straight ahead and clutched the edge of the dashboard. "You can take your gawddamned, sonabitching circus and—shove it!!!"

"Well!" she said, shocked. "I never zought you'd talk like zat to me."

"Your circus is getting to me." I scowled, still looking straight ahead. Somehow, I couldn't face her. I was that angry. I was also ready to cry. "Besides, you should hear Tina when she loads the animals up at night."

"But I don't expect zat kind of language out of you. Can't you control yourself?"

Then I realized—I had lost control! That scared me worse than the possibility that she would fire us both. It would be all my fault!

I went back to the bus in tears. For a long time, I just sobbed and shrieked and howled. Nobody but the dog could hear me. Shadow sat in front of me, licking away the salty tears.

Later, I made a sign and hung it on the door. It said I quit because we had a bunch of crybabies on the crew.

All night long, I lay awake thinking up another sign. I was hung up on signs like some people are about writing notes to themselves. The new sign would say:

> This vehicle is owned by Terry
> Erickson and is not employed by
> any other source. All services
> are guaranteed or money will be
> refunded. Any complaints to
> anyone else except directly to
> the Pie Car Manager will not be
> recognized.

Then I added:

> You better gripe to God because
> He's the only one I'll take orders
> from!

Who the hell did I think I was? Where was my humility? I remember Red saying you had to have humility to be on a circus. I couldn't be acting this way. I was alienating all of them and there was no functioning outside the gate.

Either you were in, or you were so far out, there was no way back. I was terrified.

As the night lengthened, gradually my anger diffused, but not the lingering depression. I told Curtis about cussing Gudrun out. He was strangely quiet but he didn't scold me.

I knew too well how much he loved that little circus. I was resolved to stick it out, no matter what. I loved Curtis and I didn't want to spoil the best time he was ever having for the whole of his lifetime. It would be difficult for me to swallow my pride, but I would for Curtis's sake.

After Palmdale, we had several dates around Bakersfield. If only we could get over the Tehachapi grade, we might find a wrecking yard with a transmission for our bus, and maybe another motor. Second gear had gone out and now there was a water leak. Curtis suspected a cracked block.

It was a long hard pull up Tehachapi grade, even though we started out on high desert. Suddenly we were cresting the top and the drop off the other side was 5% grade! I held my breath. We were moving very fast—down—down to the valley floor below! Curtis didn't want to use the brakes. If all four wheels weren't grabbing we could burn them up. We were going too fast to change to lower gears, so we rode off that mountain like a runaway Diesel with a severed air hose.

One thing was sure—if we couldn't find a new motor and transmission, the only way we could make it to the end of the season was—if it was all downhill.

10

Morning found us in Lamont beside a schoolyard with a fenceful of children peering eagerly at our gay red and white circus trucks.

"Where's the elephant?"

"Do you have a tiger?"

"When does the tent go up?"

The principal came over and shooed the children back to their classrooms.

Then, when they were out of earshot, he asked the very same questions.

"Can you find out when they're going to put up the tent? There are no windows on the principal's office and—" His eyes begged me to see the little boy.

I sent Billy to ask Jay. Billy returned. "About forty-five minutes," he said very importantly.

In forty-five minutes all the classes had been lined up and marched across the field to the tent site. Curtis, like a Pied Piper, was in the lead. He was explaining what had to be done.

Neena pulled on the center pole. She went down on her front knees and balanced herself with her trunk.

Jay yelled, "Go, Neena!"

Neena pulled and tugged. Slowly, the center pole raised the canvas up off the ground. The children all clapped and Neena took a bow. Ron had her pose and stand on her hind feet. Neena trumpeted a thank you to the children. They squealed in delight.

As the children began to file back toward their classrooms, one child yelled out, "Look! The flag fell!"

The centerpole flag had fallen. Quickly, Peewee hoisted Billy on his shoulders and placed him on the edge of the half-erected tent. Billy scampered to the top amid cheers from the children. With shouts and screams they urged the little four-year-old boy on as he retrieved the flag and struggled to set it in place. But he couldn't get the flag pole to match up to the centerpole tip.

Peewee jumped for the edge of the canvas and hoisted himself along the new stitching of the centerpiece where the canvas was the strongest. Carefully, he worked his way along until he reached his son. As Peewee helped Billy raise Old

Glory, the kids shouted chants of praise. They were clapping as wildly as for a returning war hero.

Peewee kissed Billy tenderly and slid down the seam. Billy turned loose, and using the canvas as a giant slide, dropped to his father's waiting arms below.

Again the children clapped. Billy was their pint-sized little Superman of the day—their own hero. Then, with a great flourish, the little grandstander turned and made a dignified bow. Big John wasn't the only ham around.

But Ron walked by in a cloud of gloom. "After what happened to Tom, I wouldn't have done that."

Maybe that's why Peewee did it. Someone had to break the superstition.

Later, Billy came by Pie Car. He had thirty-five cents and wanted another egg. I always painted the boiled eggs. Today I had clowns. Tomorrow, maybe I would go back to roses. Once I had painted marijuana plants on one batch, but nobody noticed. No one commented on my clowns, either, except Billy. There was a Lou Jacobs clown with a big long head. The Kelly clown had a downturned mouth and a red nose. There were white-faced clowns of all faces.

Billy loved clowns and begged to "read" my big clown book again. When he tired of looking at the pictures, he investigated the bus. It always fascinated him. There were so many things to ask questions about. He fingered my hot pad that had a picture of Jesus on it and a saying.

There was little religion, if any, on the show. Once Billy swore, "Oh God!"
I said, "Don't say that to God unless you're going to pray to Him."
He looked bewildered.
"Do you know what praying means?"
He didn't answer.
"Praying is when you talk to God," I said. "But you can't see Him."
Billy looked like I lost him there. "You know," I said, determined to make my point, "when they turn the generator on, we get electricity, but you can't see it, can you?"
He agreed.
"But you believe it's there, don't you? Else how could Carmen make popcorn?"
He understood that.
"God is like electricity. You know something is there when you throw the switch." I realized I had gone too far. I didn't try to explain what the God-switch was.

I showed him a picture of Jesus. I was telling him about the man from Nazereth when one of the Riveras came to the door for a cold soda. Billy busied himself with the clown book.

"That's Lou Jacobs!" he cried out.

Funny. That kid instantly knew who Lou Jacobs was by his makeup.

After Billy left, I began to put on my own makeup for the first show. I thought how rich and full my life was right now, despite the rigors of the road. It seemed to me as if I had always been following an elephant van down the road. If the performers were distant, and still considered us to be First-of-May or people who only stayed a few weeks and when the going got rough, quit, nonetheless, I had accepted my circus life. I had succeeded in making friends with Billy and Neena and Sparky the dog, not to mention the little Pygmy goats. I was on good footing with Peewee and Bob, too.

Then there were all those sticky little hands I stamped with my elephant stamp every night.

I was busy taking tickets and stamping hands that night when I noticed my very real elephant at the edge of the front door canvas, peeking around the corner and swinging her trunk.

"Hi, Neena," I said. She lifted her trunk up in a greeting.

"Neena!" I shrieked. The only reason she could be exactly where she was standing was if she had gotten loose again.

I looked to the ground. This time there was no mistake. First came the elephant, then came the chain, but no stake—no stake in the ground. She had pulled it loose and was taking herself an evening stroll.

I moved very fast, yelling back at some responsible adults standing nearby. "Keep away from her!" I flew into the tent and grabbed Jay, who was working the concessions. "Neena's loose again!"

I was afraid he wouldn't believe me after I had cried 'wolf' so many times, but, thank goodness, he followed after me.

Before we could get back on the midway, Neena had speedily trotted down to the far end of the field. I don't know where she was going, but wherever it was, she was going there fast.

Jay brought her back and herded her into her van. Poor Neena! She had been having so much fun. Why did I always have to play the rat-fink and snitch on her?

The rest of the night was a mess. We got a bunch of rowdies who only wanted to harass the paying customers. Finally, with the help of the candy butchers, we drove them away. I didn't know until later that they had circled back around the tent and tried to ignite the far corner. It was a good thing the canvas had been sprayed with flame retardant.

I was spitting mad. The circus was to enjoy. It was for kids, six or sixty. Any child under twelve could even see the show free. Tons of free ducats were handed out every week in schools and through businesses.

Most of the rowdies looked under twelve. All they had to do was pick up a free pass at the Seven-Eleven and walk right in. Why would they want to destroy a circus?

We had enough destroying factors. Not only did we have financial trouble, breakdowns, bad weather, but as far as Curtis and I were concerned, even though we wanted to continue on with all our hearts, the old bus with its sick little engine was sobbing out its last breath.

We had traveled with the circus for over a month. We had frozen, roasted, nearly blown away, sat in mud and cried in aching frustration, but we kept on the move. Then came the day when the engine wouldn't take any more punishment and we were stranded—left behind by the circus.

We faced a big decision. We could quit, leave the show and find jobs, or—we could get a loan, get the bus fixed and catch up with them. I knew the old rule, but I didn't know how it could apply to us now. With a broken down bus, a sleazy mechanic, an untested motor, another loan to be paid off, and yet—the show must go on.

I was restless without the circus. By 6:30 am, after fitfully sleeping off and on all night, I awoke thinking I heard the reel truck's heartthrob whine as its diesel engine belched to life in clouds of smoke. Somewhere up the line, my circus was waking up. Red would stretch and crawl out of his cocoon in the truck cab. His clothes would be more wrinkled than ever for his having slept in them—his precious battered old hat cocked over his eyes. He'd light up a cigarette, smoke it, cough, blink his eyes at the early morning light and shiver from the cold. Then he would climb back up in the cab and revv up that throbbing, pulsating diesel motor.

Like the giant heart of the tent, that motor beat faster with the passion it had for life—for that circus performance and all those children. It was Red's heart beating in unison—one circus indivisible, one purpose—a show for the kids, one love—a tent full of happy, well-entertained children.

There is no dollar.

There is no other world, only circus.

There is no other way, except to be free to roll down the road at night to the next town.

The reel truck would wake the others up. Men in work clothes would pour out of the sleeper bus. Far out on some athletic field or fairgrounds, Red and Bryan would lay out a conformation of stakes.

It would begin to rain. Bryan and Red would shiver but continue making the dye marks for the stakes. Carlos would skulk around mumbling. Unlike his usual cheerful self, he reacted to the rain like a long-haired cat.

Then the stakes were driven. Sledgehammers rang. Men chanted a cadence as every third blow became his to drive. They called a hundred year old chant. They pounded the stakes. They lifted hammers and cursed the hard ground. They were no longer cold as sweat formed brown stains on the backs of their shirts. Shirts came off. Bare backs glistened with sweat. Muscles rippled across broad shoulders. Hard work drew the men closer together—one union indivisible of shit-shoveling, backbending, sonsobitches who didn't know there was any other way of life.

Now the reel truck unrolls its precious cargo. Canvas bags lie lifelessly limp on the uneven ground, still folded, still damp from the night air. In unison, the men grab the edges and unfold the tent. Sections of faded canvas rise in the air as tent poles are hoisted in place. Sides rise up, leaving the center slack.

Ron gets Neena out of her van. With her heavy work harness around her massive shoulders, Neena shoves under the tent, pulling the long center pole up into place. It wedges tight. She drops to her knees to get traction, balancing her body with her trunk. Two tons of pachydermic power tugs at the pole until it will go no further.

Now, with the center pole erect and all the quarter poles in place, the tent comes alive. Billowing out with puffs of cold air, the canvas draws taut as men lean against the guy ropes, pulling with all their strength, tugging together, calling out chants in unison, until the tent is securely moored.

The wind picks up and unfurled flags above rat-tat-tat in brisk early morning gusts.

The men stop work. It's break time—time for coffee and fried pies, perhaps a bowl of scrambled eggs and a buttered muffin—time for Bryan's beer.

This morning, Red won't have his coffee. Bryan won't have a cold beer.

Cliff and Daryl won't have their regular three-egg omelets with everything but the kitchen sink thrown in. Carlos won't have his usual two big glasses of cold milk. Jay will stomp around, watching his horses nibbling bits of hay, feeling hunger gnawing at his own stomach, ignoring it Spartanly till later. There is too much to do to go off to the Seven-Eleven.

Then I remembered the route sheet. Tonight was a cold date—no sponsor.

At least not a working one because the charity was for the blind. I wondered who would take my place on the door.

11

My hair was stiff with dust and grime, probably polluted California rain.

Most of all, I had been two weeks without a shampoo. I remember my mother rubbing corn meal into my hair when I had the measles and my hair couldn't be washed. Or was it the Chicken Pox?

I seriously considered dumping a box of corn meal over my head. The worst that could happen would be for it to start raining again and turn me into a hush puppy. Come to think of it—mama and the corn meal—it was her fur coat she cleaned, not my hair.

I slept soundly through a prophet's 8.8 earthquake. I wouldn't have felt it anyway. I thought the ad I had read in the local newspaper was really weird. It had said:

> To Christians, Jew and others
> who will listen. The Lord has
> warned me in a dream that there
> will be an 8.8 earthquake in S.F.
> April 2 at 3:02 am.

High winds buffeted the bus like a sloop in a gale. I wouldn't know an earthquake if I were straddling the San Andreas fault.

Then there was the early morning rocking. The show took bets on which vehicle swayed the most—Peewee's van or our bus. Even the slightest movement sent my hanging pots, pans, ladles, can opener and tin cups into a melodious tinkling like wind chimes in a stiff breeze. Early morning in Curtis's arms was like a Force 5 storm. So much for our lovemaking.

Despite all the hardships, we were happy, terribly in love and none of the show troubles or our own breakdown could diminish our own happiness. We were warm and comfortable in the bus as the days flew by.

Things weren't as smooth back at winter quarters. Beautiful Gudrun, the boss's wife, was in a high fettle. When Curtis called in, she reported all three trucks were bogged down in mud at King City. Like a seraphic seer I had predicted another tow bill as I saw the rains continuing. I wondered if the same thing would happen in Greenfield. It probably would unless they tented on asphalt.

"We hire you to stay with the show," Gudrun fumed in her thick German accent. "You were supposed to have a reliable vehicle!"

"She's being unreasonable as usual," I spit out when Curtis repeated the conversation. "I would assume that Sandy, who has to put up arrows or everyone gets lost, should have the most reliable vehicle of all. Her van is still tied up in the shop. Only in some hick town like this would it take all week to weld up a gas tank."

"That's why Gudrun's so hostile. Her fight isn't with us."

"Maybe we're out for a week ourselves, but at least we aren't costing the show $80 a whack to tow us out of the mud! If I were running this show, I'd put an electric winch with a power take-off and three hundred foot of steel cable on the front of this bus. Then I'd sit there with it out of gear, brace myself against a tree and pull the van, the reel truck and the sleeper all out of the mud. They could then get stuck as many times as they wanted to."

I really had up a head of steam. We had been disappointed from the very start. We'd have never signed on if we'd known we were intended to be nothing more than intelligent looking flunkies. We'd been hired to be office managers. So far, we hadn't been allowed to manage as much as one of the Pygmy goats.

I remembered back in Arizona when the whole show was bogged down in the mud. I asked Curtis if there was anything he could do to help. "Honey," Curtis said, "it's important that I do nothing to undercut Red's authority. You know I spent fifteen years in South America on back roads. I could get those trucks out.

"So could John if he were here. But I described to John how I would do it, and he said, 'I can't take Red off. He's the manager.' Red's not asking me for advice."

"How about the donikers?" I added, knowing we were only comforting each other in the wake of Gudrun's verbal assault. Nothing was going to get changed. "Why couldn't we save a lot of money for the show by mounting two donikers on our trailer, maybe even a portable shower and hot water heater? Those donikers cost a hundred dollars a stand because we have to rent the toilets by the week. For six days they stand unused after we move on."

Curtis shook his head. "Who's going to tow the toilets?"

So much for traveling donikers.

I sat down and made a long list of suggested improvements for the show.

I handed them to Curtis. He looked them over and tore them up. "Who's going to tell Gudrun?"

So much for antiquated 1869 mud shows.

It was past noon. The mechanic hadn't shown up. Curtis said it would cost another three hundred and fifty dollars to have the job done right. I blew up.

That took every penny we had, what I had borrowed, what I had saved from my Pie Car profits and our last paycheck. We wouldn't be getting a paycheck for our "down" time. We'd be flat broke and stranded out in the middle of nowhere. But I finally gave in.

Curtis called another mechanic. He was sure this man would be reliable. When the mechanic showed up, he took us to a wrecking yard in his pickup. The first engine we bought had to be exchanged. The first mechanic had given us bad advice.

However, I was in a good mood. At least we were making some progress now—that is until Curtis returned with a check for three hundred and eighty dollars. We had paid four seventy-five for the first motor, flywheel and bell housing. Brazenly, the wrecking yard attendant claimed they discounted all returns. They had also guaranteed that the motor would fit "as is," but the mechanic started naming off all the other things that would have to be replaced in order to convert to a 390 engine. The mechanic we had with us this time had found another motor at another yard that would do the job. But more money would be needed.

At that point, I blacked out. We had been *had*! I fled down the street on foot with Curtis following after me pleading for me to be reasonable.

"No!" I screamed through a faceful of tears. "Leave me alone! Go back! Go back!" People were watching. I raised my voice even louder. I didn't care whether they thought he was a rapist or not. "Go back to the pickup, your mechanic, your motor—your bus! I wash my hands of the whole deal—of the circus, and our marriage too!"

Curtis was stunned. Finally he just stopped in the middle of the street and let me continue walking. I didn't look back. Now I wasn't blinded by tears. I was blind with rage. I wanted to hide. No! I wanted to run away!

Then I saw a garage sale at a mini-storage lot. No one would think of looking for me in such an obvious place. Evidently someone had failed to pay storage dues. Now their possessions were being sold. That might happen to our things, if the rent wasn't met where we had stored our belongings. If I didn't have a job or a husband, how would I ever see my things again? And what about my brand new twelve hundred dollar IBM Selectric typewriter?

I tried to force the fear and panic down by pretending to read book titles.

My heart was still pounding fiercely. I touched racks of clothing. I bought a book about the movies, one of those picture kinds that end up conversational pieces on a coffee table. Then I found a music box with the head of a clown. I wound it up and it played "Send in the Clowns."

Then I realized—I couldn't leave the circus and I certainly couldn't leave Curtis. He was my whole life! How could I have hurt him so? How could I have run away from him? He was so dear and precious to me!

I hitchhiked a ride back to town and asked to be dropped off in front of the bank. My son had been sending money home regularly and I had been putting it into my own personal savings account for him. There was nothing else I could do now but borrow from his money. Somehow I would find a way to put it back before he came home on furlough from the army.

I planned to give Curtis the money, all right, but I wasn't going to take the matter of the unscrupulous junkyard gypping us without a fight. After I left the bank, I walked down to the Chamber of Commerce where I told them my story—how one of their upstanding citizens had ripped us off.

Suddenly I was terribly worried about Curtis. He didn't have any idea where I was or what had happened to me. All I wanted to do was get back to my bus, to Curtis's loving arms, to my dog and my Teddy Bear!

I called and left word at the butane place next door to the field where we were broken down. They knew who I was and said they would take a message out to the bus. In minutes, Curtis called back.

"I really thought of splitting," I said over the phone. "I could've called my daughter, Donna, you know. She would've come and gotten me."

But Curtis said the magic words. "I fixed him. He forgot to list the bell housing on the receipt, so I kept it."

That night, as I wound up my music box clown and looked at the pictures in my movie star book, I said, "How come you didn't get worried? I really could have run away."

"Maybe," he said calmly, "but you'd come back for your dog and your Teddy Bear."

12

I had little else to do but sit and watch TV. Johnny Carson interviewed Casey Jones, who was 110 years old. Johnny asked him to what did he attribute his successfully long life.

"Be happy," Mr. Jones said, with a twinkle in his eye, "and do the things you want to do."

Half the time I didn't know what I wanted to do. I thought that chasing around the country with a little broken-down, one-elephant mud show was a grand adventure. Now I was confused. The only thing that really mattered was being secure in Curtis's arms every night. That could be done anywhere.

I thought I wanted to become a clown. For a while, it was an obsession. I drew clown pictures in my diary. I dabbed a lot of makeup on my face, only to quickly clean it off before someone saw me.

We were parked in front of the house of the mechanic. He rebuilt the motor mounts and set the transmission in. He was an architect, but without a house to build recently, he fell back on his skill as a mechanic. While he worked on our bus, I entertained his children.

My first crude attempt at clowning was successful as far as the kids were concerned. My face was made up nicely. With my own hair up in messy puppy dog tails, it looked like a fright wig. I drew my eyebrows into high arched vees with black pencil, smeared red lipstick on my nose and dotted my cheeks bright pink. Now I was Kookie, the Klown.

Even Curtis approved, but it didn't push away that horrible feeling that, try as I might to be "circus," our future was in jeopardy.

Curtis called winter quarters. Gudrun was full of dire threats. She had to drive all the way up to replace us. I could hear that thick German voice thundering—"Fire those unreliable Ericksons!"

"Didn't you tell her that if anyone would have helped us, from Red on down, we might've gotten on the road a week sooner?"

"I didn't get a chance." Curtis slumped into silence.

"Curtis, you have to tell them! If you don't, the whole show'll hate us for being quitters! As it is, they're so afraid of you becoming active manager that they're trying to freeze us out."

"Everyone had an excuse."

"Not one person would help you, you mean."

"I asked Marian. She said she couldn't drive into town because she had to put on her makeup and take a nap."

"And the others?"

"One by one, they all begged off."

"I can't believe absolutely everyone on the show refused to help you find a mechanic."

"Bryan said he would, but Tina took off with Sandy in the bear van. Curtis Cainian probably would've helped, but he had his own troubles with the transmission out in His pickup."

"Did you tell Big John all of this, and that we couldn't even rent a car or get a cab because there wasn't one in the whole town?"

"No. He probably thought we could at least hire a cab."

"Did you also tell him that you found one mechanic the very next day after we broke down, gave him a hundred dollars in advance and the guy went off on a lost weekend?"

"No."

"And how about that you hired a second mechanic who didn't show up at all because he, too, was drowning his troubles?"

"No, I didn't get a chance. Big John came through here on his way to the next stand, but he didn't stop or seem to want to get involved. You know, every man for himself."

"He warned you he wasn't picking up any repair bills. I guess he thought if he stopped, we'd put the bite on him for the bill."

"The trouble with this outfit," he said, "is no communication."

"That's exactly why you have to tell him what really went wrong." I began the dirge. We ran out of ideas. Then the crooked wrecking yard owner ripped us off, sold us the wrong-sized motor and, all the prices quoted to us by local garages were over our head.

"Nevertheless, John said that if we had any more breakdowns, we were fired."

"Breakdowns are totally unpredictable."

"We've already used up our quota."

"John doesn't care. He's a fast freight train, rushing through town, not caring whether there's cows on the track or not, just as long as he has a good cowcatcher up front."

"No," Curtis objected. "John's being as reasonable as he can. I have to be at that pay window every show from now on, no matter what. If we break down, I have to leave you and Shadow with the bus, but I have to make it."

"You wouldn't leave me!" I gasped.

"I won't leave you." He kissed me.

When I put aside my worries about breaking down and getting canned off the show, the stay in Atascadero was quite pleasant. We had little to do while the mechanic finished installing the 350 Camaro engine. Regardless of what kind of a reception we got when we would finally catch up with the show, Curtis and I were happy in our old bus.

The mechanic was nearly finished. Only one more part had to be installed, and that was the drive shaft. It didn't fit. Such a minor thing but it held us up one more day.

"Why can't you and the mechanic find a welder?"

"We did."

"Then why can't he go ahead and shorten the drive shaft so Dennis can finish up and get us on our way?"

"Because the welder's snake has a sore throat."

"WHAAAAAT!" I shrieked.

"Yeah," Curtis smiled. "The welder has a pet snake with a sore throat and he had to take it to the vet's."

The drive shaft was in by noon. Curtis called Yucaipa and told John we would make it to Avenal by the six o'clock showtime. We had to cover over a hundred miles with a totally untried motor and transmission but they decided to hold together. In fact, they fairly sang going down the road.

Curtis ordered me not to worry any more about the Pie Car. If we had to, we'd throw the twenty-eight dollars worth of pies in the garbage and write off the loss. Mattel was losing millions on Circus World. I could afford to lose a few pies.

We made Avenal by 5 P.M., but Pie Car business was way off that night. Pies weren't the only loss. Cliff had been fired. He had been my best customer.

We had become good friends. He even gave me a tiny flagon of gold dust and two little hand stamps to use on the kids at the door. On his birthday, I gave him a key ring that lit up like a tiny flashlight. Afterwards, I wondered if he carried keys. There were no locks on canvas. Towners always carried keys, but roustabouts and circus workmen are often ex-hoboes. Hoboes don't have any need for keys—no doors. I wondered if Red had ever been a hobo?

Just then, Red walked by the Pie Car. Curtis asked him why no one was eating at Pie Car since we returned to the show.

"I guess they got out of the habit," he said.

Habit! Every night, the same music is played, Red gives the same spiel on the midway, Neena walks round and round giving rides to children. Every night, the dogs perform the same tricks, the ponies walk around their ring, the clowns do the same stale gags two performances a day, seven nights a week, eight months a year!

Habit! How do you teach an old circus performer new tricks? How do you break them of going to the Seven-Eleven? Maybe Curtis and I should start eating there, too. I would, but I'd be afraid I'd be sick.

I was settling down to habitual patterns myself. Curtis asked me, "Are you happy?"

"You know I'm happy. You understand?"

"Yes, or you wouldn't still be here."

"I guess women have gotten themselves in worse messes."

"Like what?" Curtis asked, amused.

"I could be on a wickiup."

"What's that?"

In love with the word, even though I didn't really know what it meant, I continued. "Can't you see me on a wickiup pulled by Neena, trying to type as I bounce down the road?"

"What do you think a wickiup is?"

"I think it's two branches hung from the back of an old horse. The Indian puts his fat old squaw on the wickiup and drags her along behind."

Curtis laughed. "I think you have it mixed up with something else. A wickiup's something like a teepee."

Some days, the men played a sort of a shell game on me about charging.

The one thing Big John had stressed when we first started out was, "Don't charge." But what could I do when the biggest charger was the boss himself, Red.

Red would charge a sandwich, pie and pop. Then two more sandwiches and a pop. He would acquire a five dollar bill somewhere so he paid Curtis off for four packages of cigarettes. (I had refused to handle cigarettes in Pie Car, so Curtis kept some in the office van.) I got the last dollar. Then Red sent Bob for another piece of pie and a hot coffee for which Bob paid cash—eighty cents. Red ended the day still owing $5.35. Tomorrow, he'd probably do the same thing.

The idea caught on. Blond-headed, enigmatic Daryl, another steady customer, came along when Red was doing his little dollar down-dollar a day routine. Daryl's tab run: Breakfast, pie and cola—$4.00. He gave me his last dollar. In a few minutes, he was back for a candy bar. He still owed me $3.50.

Edward, Carlo's half-brother, joined the circus. He listened to the breakfast shell game and joined in the fun. I was tired of adding and subtracting.

"Look," I said, exasperated. "Either it's charge it all, or nothing at all. No bookwork!"

Edward looked at his pie and coffee, dug into his grimy workpants for change and plunked down exactly eighty cents. I had spoiled all the fun.

Some days were sweeter than others. Somewhere out there beyond our tent was a world full of people, fighting each other, feeling miserable, quarreling and dying. Our life on the show was so peaceful. I looked out over the field. There was my friendly old tent. Bob was behind the sideshow car folding up his illusion box.

I walked up behind him with a big grin and said, "Have I told you how much I love you and my little circus?" It scared the daylights out of him. I walked away, picking up candy wrappers as I went and throwing them in the dumpster.

But not everybody on the circus was as happy.

The three clowns were gloomy and miserable. The more unhappy they became in their personal loneliness, the funnier their acts were.

Only Neena seemed content as she followed Peewee to water. She trumpeted across the parking lot in sheer pleasure, bobbing along behind the only man she loved.

Peewee, with his long blond hair cropped shoulder length, looked like a Dutchman. Maybe he was. Carmen was from Belgium. Peewee was handsome in a rough cut, broad shouldered, slim hipped way. Apart from my own husband, I thought Peewee was the sexiest guy on the show. Carmen, his wife, did too.

Some people go to church on Sunday, but circus people go to bed. Our eight hour day begins about four P.M. and goes on till after midnight. Then there is the "commute" after that. This week, we get off easy—only thirty-mile hops between stands.

"You were the first ones there, huh?" Red said over his morning coffee.

I thought—that's his way of reversing the complaint. Never again would we be dragging in last, now that we had the "Camaro" bus.

13

I watched fannies. Tina walked by, as firm as a brick factory. Sandy walked by—a bigger brick factory with all the bricks stacked on the lower end.

I should talk. I was a whole brick Pentagon.

I smarted when Bob picked on Sandy. "I know how she diets—on M&Ms," he said. I did too.

I asked Curtis how come they rode Sandy about getting fat and not me. He said, "She's an athlete. Sandy's been a performer since she was a child. She's expected to keep herself in shape."

It was about 6:30 A.M., and it was raining. The ritual began. My dog barked. Through opaque drapes I could see the shadowy figure approaching—broad shoulders, trim waist, hunched over against the cold—funny, floppy old hat. I didn't need to see the red, white, blue of him to know it was Red Johnson.

Red walked away. He feared Shadow, my Doberman. It was part of the ritual. First the dog barked. Then I came to the rescue. I yelled across to him. "I'll have the coffee warm in a minute!"

More ritual. I hauled the dog's chain in with it rattling against the side of the bus like all the demons in hell turned loose. That would wake the whole circus up. Then I chained my ferocious, tail-wagging fake in the rear of the bus, out of my way.

Soggy, shivering Red slipped in the door and dropped thirty cents on the table.

"Red," I said, pouring his coffee, "have you ever played this wet a year?"

In that stupendously profound spiel voice, gravelly and monotone—the same voice that announced the weirdoes, the freaks, the three-legged man—Bozo, the dogfaced boy, the man who drives ice picks through his skull—Red said, "Never, It's always spring by now."

"I think this has been the worst winter ever."

"You missed the real bad weather the week you were gone. We lost three trucks in the mud."

I didn't answer. I knew about it. I had posted the tow bills. I hadn't gone away, just remained in Atascadero till I got a new motor and transmission. I didn't desert you! I wanted to cry out. All the sloshing around in the mud with them wouldn't have helped at all. But I understood now how the show felt about us. We weren't with them in their darkest hour. Somehow that made us outcasts. The schoolyard where we were to play was barren. It stood desolate in a huge pool of rainwater. Thank God for all the green grass. Maybe at least there would be some solid ground to stake the canvas in.

I couldn't see beyond the bus but I envisioned Red, Bryan and Curtis Cainian huddled together like generals of war, planning their strategy, making mysterious blue paint exxes on the athletic field to mark where the tent stakes would be driven. But the familiar jungle throb of the big truck's motor was silent this morning. It was as if the "cat" could crawl back asleep and forget the dripping skies, the penetrating cold and the soggy field.

So much for soggy Saturdays in Springtime.

They drifted in all day, partly to get out of the rainy wind. Marian came for soup and stayed through sandwiches and pie. She was almost jovial.

"You know, I told him to blow it out his pants," she said. "And you know—he did." I never did catch who she was jabbering about.

That night, after the show, we remained on the same lot overnight instead of moving on. There were high winds all night, not fit to drive in and reports of dangerous flooding to the north where our route was taking us. But after it being cold all day, the evening was mild. The boys from the sleeper all split for town where they shared the cost of a motel and a hot bath. Then, the dull gray morning's silence was pierced by the purr of the big truck. Red came by to let us know he was pulling out.

Marian and her merry men passed by under my window, all bright-eyed, bushy-tailed and well-scrubbed. To get a bath was worth having to get up at the crack of dawn to move on.

It was then I felt a distinct sadness—not the somber weather, not the leaving of this lovely park where at least we had an electrical hookup, but as the trucks pulled out, one by one, without us, and Curtis still lay in sound sleep, I realized that today was Easter Sunday.

Each morning I woke up in a different town. These were quiet mornings after so much storm. Warmed by the early spring sun sparkling from the late winter rains, the countryside enjoyed a silence broken only by the motor sound of an occasional pickup going by.

Word had gotten back from winter quarters that everyone on the circus was now satisfied with our performance. I wondered who had stopped bitching. Curtis made the right change, swept the office out and did the posting. Ever since I cussed Gudrun out, her attitude toward me changed. She didn't try to give me any more suggestions how to run Pie Car. Besides, it wasn't referred to as the Pie Car any longer. Everyone called it *The* Bus.

The first sign that we were finally being accepted as part of the show was when Sherry, Curtis Cainian and Marian came around with a basket of Easter eggs. Mine had a big raisin-studded cookie on it and the name Terry. They all called me Cookie. Curtis's egg had a dollar bill and a few coins drawn on it and his name.

As soon as they left, the mail arrived. With it a huge credit card bill for gasoline, a dun from my son in Korea for two hundred dollars of his money I'd already spent and—my clown makeup I'd secretly ordered.

Instinctively, I felt this was not the time to spring it on everyone. I put the makeup away in the drawer without even opening it. The right time would come when they needed me—when all the clowns by some misfortune couldn't go on and they were desperate.

I don't know why I was down on myself again. Maybe it was the slow, insidious addiction to chocolate cookies. I was putting on weight again and I had no room to spare.

I began talking to myself, contriving up excuses. The next time some brat asked me at the door if I was the Fat Lady, I would really mouth off.

"I used to be the Fat Lady with another circus," I would lie, "but I went to Weightwatchers and I lost so much weight, they fired me."

The real truth was I only had another two hundred pounds to go and I could be billed in the sideshow tent as *Tiny Terry, the Terrific Fat Lady*. The sideshow needed a jolt, but I needed more. I needed to feel a part of the circus *without* being a sideshow freak. I had an important job. Someone had to take the tickets and control the crowds, ushering them around. Even if I didn't have the Pie Car, I still had a paying job on the circus. I would have gladly exchanged all of my paychecks for knowing I was really "circus."

Red was all circus. He must have been born that way. I watched him work.

Out across the field, the tent lay stretched out upon the ground. Centerpoles were being lifted in place by Neena. The men began tugging at the canvas.

Red took his place among the men. From a distance, he looked like a football player about to make a tackle. Close up, he looked lean and muscled. His back and shoulders were straight and young as if he had a coat hanger still in his shirt.

Even in grubby workpants torn at the knee, Red was a flag of color—red carrot hair, white Irish skin, blue, blue eyes, the color of agate marbles—the color of Ron's white cat's one eye.

He lifted the canvas effortlessly. Like a lead horse in a team of draft Percherons, Red demonstrated how light the canvas was, how pleasant it was to bust one's ass lifting and tugging it, how beautiful was the sweet sting of sweat in your eyes!

Red was the circus manager. Like Christ washing the feet of his disciples, Red led the circus by example. He had their respect.

The next day was even more cheerful. All around, the circus sights and sounds were particularly charming.

Four little ponies were tethered to the reel truck. Tina was shoveling shit in nothing but a loincloth—her costume for the Princess Moonbeam number. An old Lion watched her from a distance, looking hungrily at the sexy kitten. He was one of the old darlings from the Lion's club who were our sponsors working the gate. Towners were lining up on the warm spring day to see the show, and Red, our flag, was "flying" colorfully from the sideshow bally platform. Bob Seaton, the magician, and Bryan, the tent boss, were playing ball in the back yard while dogs in ruffled collars stood by watching, tethered on short little leashes.

That afternoon, Mike and his wife, a couple we had met at the laundromat, showed up for the matinee. Mike was covered with tattoos, every inch of him tattooed in ornate detail. He asked for a job.

"Your wife would have to work, too," I said.

"She's very good with horses."

"How about snakes?" I was thinking about Charlie, the boa constrictor who wanted to join the show in Coalinga.

"She loves snakes," he said, completely throwing me off guard. "Her pet garter snake just died."

"What happened?"

"We gave it a fish," he said sadly. "It choked to death. I didn't know it would hurt it."

"There's a big difference between a garter snake and a boa constrictor. The fish wouldn't have hurt a boa constrictor." I paused and watched his face. His wife was over at the concession trailer buying popcorn and was out of earshot. "Does she like boa constrictors?"

"Sure." Then he added timidly, "How long?"

"Seven feet."

"Geez! He could eat a live chicken!"

"I don't know. We haven't bought him yet. Think it over and see me after the show."

I told Jim about the tattooed man and his wife, the snake lady. Jim got all excited and ran to tell Red.

"They're just what we need for that sick side show."

Red exploded. "Sounds great, but who do I fire? We have a full payroll."

Half the time the show can't hardly make payroll as it is!" His face was a thundercloud about to burst.

"Couldn't he somehow get a percentage?"

"I'm not giving up my cut." Red stomped off stubbornly.

Jim smiled. "It's still a good idea. It'd really bring in the crowd."

"Can't Red see that a better side show would generate more money to split?"

"I guess not."

"With the snake, the crowd would have something live to see—something wiggling and moving."

"Hey, what about me?" Jim said. He sounded hurt.

"You know what I mean. It's a weak show in there. Half the time you have to be out front spieling for Red."

It was true. Jim was an excellent juggler and he wanted time to practice a new routine, but there wasn't any spare time. All morning, he busted ass on the canvas, then most of the day it was "fetch these," "fix this," "wire that up," until he barely had time to get ready for his opening number. Between shows, he had to stand by to replace Red every time the boss was called off in another direction.

Then, to top that off, every other night, Jim had to drive the sleeper from town to town. Red knew that Jim didn't drink and was seriously dedicated to the show. He was one of those riser-uppers who planned on going someplace. So Red worked him to death. It wasn't Red's fault. That was the circus way. If you wanted to make it in the circus, you worked till you dropped and then you volunteered for more. The one who worked the cheapest and longest got the pot, the gold and the gaudy rainbow at the end of the midway.

I looked down our midway to see Curtis wildly waving in my direction. I couldn't hear him shouting over the cacophonous sounds of the midway. I went over to his ticket window.

"Don't you know Jim's mike is still on? We can hear every word you're say-ing—arguing over there about hiring the tattooed man."

I felt like crawling in a gopher hole. Now I was in for it. If Red overheard our conversation, he would again think I was trying to run the show.

"But it's still a good idea, Curtis. You heard me tell him about the tattooed man and his wife who was willing to work snakes? That's just what this flunky outfit needs. Maybe Mike could throw knives at his wife, too, or swallow swords. I'm sure he can learn to do fire."

14

Sparks of flame shot forth from a ragged electric cord. I looked down the midway. A small boy was swinging on the first light pole on the midway.

I yelled, "Don't do that! You'll turn off the light and somebody'll fall in a hole!"

He looked up at me innocently with huge blue eyes. "Will the Devil in the hole get 'em?"

I looked around the midway quickly, remembering I'd just seen a huge tent spike hole. Finding it by the side canvas, I showed the hole to the little boy.

"See that hole?" I said, tongue in cheek. "You stand right there and watch it carefully. Let me know when the Devil sticks his head out."

Last I saw he was still watching the hole. The light pole was left undisturbed for the rest of the evening.

Towners were always trying to be helpful. That's probably how the idea of the "auguste" clown came about. This one fellow applied for a job who called himself Cash. He didn't look like he'd seen much of it in his lifetime. Cash talked like a night freight train rumbling across a trestle, with no water stops. If he could work like he talked, the canvas would be on the reel in forty-five minutes.

At first, I thought he was circus naive like most towners. I gave him a Glad bag and told him teardown began with cleaning up the midway. Actually, the job of tidying up the midway had fallen on my shoulders, just because I happened to be in the right spot at the wrong time. Everybody was busy tearing down when the litter had to be gathered up, except for me.

Cash walked away with his bag. I thought he'd really fallen for it. Then I looked up and saw he had requisitioned the next idle kid standing around and passed the Glad bag on.

For a while, it looked like we had another "paper house." Six schoolteachers, holding a pass given to them by our advance man, Jamie, approached the gate. Following them were fifty school children with free passes. That meant fifty-six people saw the circus free on one lousy V.I.P. pass!

Red turned apoplectic pink. A little while later, Bob asked for the ticket sacks so he could count the Day-of-Shows. The tickets were coming through fast. I couldn't really estimate the Day-of-Shows—tickets given out virtually at the last minute. To add to it, the advance sales got all screwed up. One lady showed up who owned a local motel. She had bought a whole fistful of advance sale tickets, contributing to the charity, which in this case was a club for the blind, and then given her tickets out as advertisement for her motel.

"The people all came back to me squawking," she moaned. "The tickets were for the next town eight miles away, and most of them didn't have any transportation!"

I apologized all over the place and guaranteed we would honor her out-of-town tickets for the second show if she could only round up all of her friends.

She returned for the second show, but no one was with her except a girl who looked like her sister. This time, she was all smiles. The last I saw of her, she was enjoying the show. When I told Red how I handled her, he seemed pleased.

Usually, the blind sponsors didn't show up except after the show to get their cut, but tonight was different. Guided by a man who was only partially blind, a woman named Linda stumbled over the end piece at the gate. Her eyes rolled and her small white hand searched for anything to steady herself. Another half-blind person furnished her with a chair and a small shopping bag.

Linda wore no makeup. Her hair hung straight and unadorned. She was beautiful even though she remained expressionless. She sat poised, listening, eager, expectant—drinking in huge draughts of exotic scents from the circus, filling her ears with sounds that produced a profusion of imagery.

Neena trumpeted. The loudspeaker blared the *Trojan March* and Jim barked his spiel down the midway.

"The circus begins over here at the old time circus side show. See Flamo the Fireeater. He can eat enough flame in a week to heat a small-sized ranch home. He's on the inside. He's alive. The human pincushion—he can stick a five-inch ice pick into his skull. He's alive."

Linda held her little bag out, the kind that usually toted bananas—one with a handle. "I'm working the gate with you," she said to me firmly.

When people handed her their tickets, she felt for what she could not see.

She felt for the family discount ticket stapled on the coupon that had been cut out of the local newspaper. She listened to what height the voice was coming from that spoke to her, whether an adult or child. I gathered a few tickets and slipped them into her bag. Then I saw that the crowd understood and began calling out their tickets and I stopped hovering over her. She'd do just fine all by herself.

Linda listened to the music. "Is that the acrobats?" she asked, smiling serenely.

"That's Sugar and Spice," I said. "Ron is dangling upside down by his knees, holding his wife Chris below him and she—Sugar—is twirling around and around by her neck. Her head is held in a velvet loop on a swivel. Now she's contorting her body back and forth in classic acrobatic position something like a ballet." I wondered if Linda even knew what a ballet looked like. "Chris is very professional. No matter how she turns, she always holds her head in such a way that her long thick blonde hair cascades down her back."

Linda sighed in pure pleasure as she envisioned Sugar twirling high above the arena by her beautiful hair.

"Ron—Spice—is her husband. He's a black man—tall, slim and very strong. He's also the elephant handler."

Linda gasped with delight as the crowd applauded. The music changed to *Deep In The Heart of Texas.*

"That's Jay Evans's music. He stomps out in white cowboy boots and a high crowned twelve-gallon hat. It has to be two gallons more because it falls down over his ears."

She laughed.

Neither Linda nor I could see the show, but I was describing it from having seen it in my mind's eye a hundred times before.

"Jay's twirling his lariat now and jumping over it. Now he's juggling his hat on the end of his nose."

The audience began clapping in tempo as Jay spun a huge lasso he called the Texas Wedding Ring around in a wider and wider circle.

"He spins that lariat in such a huge circle that it's almost as big as the center ring."

I watched Linda's face. She seemed very intelligent. She stepped out sure-footed, not hesitant like many blind people. Stumbling blind people was a stereotype. It was what most people expected. Linda didn't stumble and she didn't quit smiling as she confidently collected the tickets and then was led away by one of her friends.

Funny thing about stereotypes. Once I went to a down-and-out rescue mission to see if I could get their truck to pick up a few things I was discarding.

"You have to return in the afternoon if you want some clothes," he said, looking me over. He thought I wanted to get some clothes, not give.

"What's wrong with the clothes I have on?" I said. I was wearing a forty-three dollar polo shirt, the most expensive one I'd ever bought.

So much for images.

Later that night, I complained bitterly to Curtis about what seemed to be a poor take. I couldn't help it. I was pushed out of shape about the way the circus was run. I couldn't understand some of the moves. For instance, we were back-tracking with the show. We were booked into a town over three hundred miles back where we had just played.

Backtracking that far with eight vehicles must be costing hundreds of dollars extra. Red booked this route. I guess hundreds of dollars in gas to give shows where at least 25% of the house was papered, is Circus. But Curtis says booking a route isn't that simple. You have to go with dates the fairgrounds are available, and things like that. The sponsors that have been with John the longest get the dates that pay best, like weekends.

Still, I couldn't see why Red booked this date. I was still angry with him about not being able to get the snake. I would've gladly bought the snake myself for the good of the show, but Curtis asked me where I proposed keeping it.

"It belongs in the side show trailer."

"Bob and Red sleep in there. I doubt it they want a seven foot boa constrictor for a roommate."

"Could we keep it under the bed?"

"Even if there was any room, I doubt if Shadow would go for the snake. You know, territorial rights and all of that."

"But the snake has his own glass tank."

"She said he also had to be kept warm."

"How do you keep a boa constrictor warm?"

"He has a hot rock that's sort of like an electric hot pad," Curtis explained, all so very seriously.

"That does it."

"Why?"

"I don't get enough electricity to refrigerate My bologna. How could I keep a snake warm?"

I didn't blame Red for not liking snakes. He ran scared like a startled rabbit. Big John was the shaggy-maned lion. Gudrun had to be a little black panther about ready to spring. Peewee was a blond ape: Daryl, a weasel with glasses, Carlos a smiling, shiny black seal waiting for his fish. Jay often looked like an old prospector's mule. Tina was a racing pony, Curtis Cainian a broken-nosed mongrel terrier and Sherry—a fancy white poodle.

I was fed up. I entertained thoughts of quitting the show. We were so sure we wanted to follow a circus wherever it went, but after six weeks on the road, I'd had enough. They were right. They were winning. We'd never be "circus."

There were lots of other things we could do. We could go back to Berkeley and write another book, or fly down to Peru to research a jungle book or go to Barcelona so Curtis could do his doctoral studies. But all of these things would take more money than we had now.

I think more than anything, I wanted to be free—free of debt, free to travel, free to get up and go to bed when and where I chose. That wasn't the circus. There was no more regimented job in the whole world unless it was being a monk in a monastery.

I remember Marian saying she was free. She looked at me and then at Curtis and said, "You're not free." I knew what she meant. She made no effort to conceal her feminist views.

But I watched her through the window when she felt all alone and free—Sam, the clown sitting sorrowfully in her pickup waiting to do Day-of-Show.

Marian was a "larry." A "larry" was a coloring book with a cover but no insides. Lovely Marian felt like there was nothing inside, only a tiny pathetic voice no one heard.

But Sam, the clown, was very much alive and loudmouthed. In the ring, no one had trouble hearing Sam's gag lines. Marian wasn't free. She was imprisoned within Sam. Or was it that Sam the clown was trapped inside Marian's female body? Somehow, I loved them both.

There were a lot of things wrong with the circus. I worried about Neena at night, locked up in that van of hers, trying to keep her balance as the van lurched down the road. She couldn't help making excrement, but she despised stepping in it. During the day when she was tethered outside, she fastidiously stepped over the sweet-scented clumps of manure that looked like miniature green bales of hay.

Like a hay compactor, the fodder went in and returned neatly packaged.

But at night, I could hear her thumping against the walls in wounded dignity. In the jungle, no one but the lion would have dared approach her. Big John, that roaring old lion, caged her.

When Neena was very young, she was trained by a man who, like John, had a drinking problem. She hated the iron hook. The trainer would gouge her in her most sensitive spot behind her ear. She could smell liquor on his breath. She hated that smell so much that even now, she became incensed when she caught wind of that odor of bad remembrances. Big John had conquered his liquor problem through Alcoholics Anonymous, and for all I knew, so had the irritable trainer. But AA didn't mean a thing to Neena. She had it firmly entrenched in her mind that the smell of booze was the smell of enemy.

One day, Curtis had a beer with his lunch. When he went by Neena on his way back to the office, she slapped him against the side of the van so hard his arm was badly bruised and skinned. After that, I always feared some drunk might try to pet her and there would be bad trouble.

The only time Neena had any freedom was in the ring. Maybe that's why she performed so well. But the time in the limelight, taking bows, having children riding her big broad back, was all too infrequent.

15

"Take Hatch Road West."

"Don't tell me east or west, just tell me left or right," Sandy said in her usual bristling lather.

"Then go to the left," Curtis explained patiently. "When you get over the overpass, turn left again on South Seventh."

That sounded clear enough. Why did I have an odd feeling of foreboding as I watched the trucks pull out one by one and head down the road?

The big rigs passed us on the freeway and disappeared on up ahead in the heavy traffic. When we got to the two Hatch Road exits—Hatch Road East and Hatch Road West, Sandy was standing at the side of the road, hastily removing her arrows from the first turnoff. With a scowl across her face as stormy as an approaching hurricane, she waved us on by.

"What do you think's the matter now, Curtis? You did explain to Sandy about the tricky Hatch Road exits, didn't you?" Even I knew you went east to get west. There was an unusual off ramp arrangement that could confuse anyone never having executed that turnoff before—like circus trucks in the middle of the night.

"I tried to. I hope she was paying attention."

"Looks very much like she didn't."

One of Curtis's jobs was to phone ahead every morning, contact the sponsor and set things up. He also asked directions. The last thing Sandy would do each night was stick her head in the office and find out where we were going so she could "do arrows." At that time of night, everyone else is busy, even Curtis, who had to be counting up the take and splitting it with the sponsors. But Sandy and Tina would leave as soon as possible in the bread van so they would be way ahead of the show. Then, while they made it to the next town, and blazed the trail, so to speak, by "doing arrows," the men would be taking the tent down, rolling it up on the huge reel, packing up and crawling out for the next stand. This took hours—usually plenty of time for Sandy to mark our way to the lot we would be playing the next day.

This time when we found the lot, even though the heavy trucks had already passed us some time back, the lot was empty. Sandy had done it again, but we'd get blamed.

"Sandy takes her arrows so seriously. Good grief! What'd she do this time?"

"Those arrows are a serious matter," Curtis said. "Most of the time I'd be lost without them to direct me. It's awfully hard to find a little circus in the middle of the night in a town you've never been in before. It just happens, I was born in Modesto."

"And I went to school here," I added.

"And we both lived here just last year." Curtis knew just how to make the difficult turn to get back on South Seventh where the auction yard was. We would be setting up the circus within five blocks of his family home. That is, if we had a circus to set up.

Three trucks were now presumed to be lost somewhere out Hatch Road East. Sandy had posted her signs at the first exit she came to, not being aware of the second turnoff that doubled back across the freeway toward the west. Before the error could be discovered, the big fast diesels were halfway to Nevada.

We got the blame, all right. The storm had begun brewing way back at the last lot. We had been late for Pie Car. The men had already eaten by the time we arrived because Chris had brought them coffee and doughnuts.

Later, I got sick on the door and asked one of the sponsors to remain the rest of the evening in my place. He guaranteed me it was okay, but as soon as I was out of sight and back in the bus, the sponsor split for the night, leaving absolutely no one guarding the door against gatecrashers and rowdies.

Red exploded. It got back to me through Curtis. I was throwing out mildewed pies, some of those bought when we had the breakdown.

"Red says, after this you stay on that door, no matter what!" Curtis wasn't mad at me. He never got mad at me, but he was upset.

I was upset too. I remembered so clearly that first night in Yucaipa when we all sat down at the kitchen table and were informed what our duties would be. There was Big John, Gudrun, Chris, Red, Curtis and me.

John had said, "Now, Curtis, what you do: you're going to represent us to the sponsors. That's why I want *you*, because you don't look like the working man. You're going to call ahead every day to the next town and make all the arrangements, find out exactly where the lot is, where they want us to put the tent up, whether there are donikers or what. Then when we get there in the morning, you have to be the first one to meet with the sponsors and make all the arrangements for collecting advance ticket sale money."

He turned to me, and in that beautiful rich voice that somehow reminded me of the Wizard of Oz, John said, "Now, Terry, you run the Pie Car. And I also want you to guarantee to be on the door when you're needed. Usually, the sponsor will work on the door, but when there's no sponsor, *you* take the tickets, Terry. The first month and a half out, there's only three dates that don't have a sponsor."

But John was wrong. It didn't work that way at all. Sponsors sometimes didn't show up until time to count the money. Other sponsors didn't know what to do. Some did it all wrong. I stayed on that door night after night because I was needed.

Red had understood John's directions differently than I had. All Red heard was the word *guarantee*. Now he was jumping all over me for letting the sponsor handle his own booking.

"He can go to hell!" I lashed back. "You told me I didn't have to work the door any time I didn't feel like it. I was hired on to run the Pie Car, not to take tickets *every* night. And I do mean every night! When we left winter quarters, Big John asked me if I wouldn't mind taking tickets once in a while when there wasn't a sponsor, which might be only twice a month. I didn't know it was going to be a cold date every night! Those sponsors are either so fucked-up old or else irresponsible, I have to take tickets anyway—even if there are a dozen of them on the gate!"

I was furious and began slamming things around the bus like a wounded wild-cat. The one thing Curtis couldn't stand was for me to lose my temper and swear. He never fought fair. He just walked away, or worse still, he tried to be reasonable with me when I wanted to be unreasonable. I wasn't mad at him. I wasn't even mad at Red. Certainly I wasn't angry with the sponsors, in general.

For the most part, they were precious old dears like the Lion's Clubs. That one irresponsible sponsor was an isolated case. I was really mad at John! But Curtis got in my way.

After the storm, came the repairing and the forgiveness. I think the worst part was the forgiveness. Curtis was always too forgiving, and I came off on the short end like a little kid who knows he deserves a good licking but the sentence is postponed.

After that, I began to get sad and melancholy, like the music from "Send In The Clowns." There were too many hours sitting in the dark with no electricity—on malls, in muddy fields, in strange towns. Anywhere, USA was always: a Safeway, Burger King, Long's Drugs, Carl's Jr., Pizza Hut and McDonald's. It was also the same blue-eyed, blond kids or dark skinned, button-eyed babies with sticky, cotton candy-covered fingers. They all held their hands up to be elephant stamped. They were all wide-eyed and excited to be seeing a circus, to hear the music and see the clowns and animals.

"Anywhere, USA" can be the loneliest place on earth when you can't ever leave to go shopping, and those little children are strangers—not one's own grandchildren.

I thought about my own grandchildren growing up without me around and I got even more depressed.

Even the interruption of one of the workmen coming to the Pie Car to buy a beer couldn't jar me from the blues.

I heard night sounds. I saw flashing red, white, blue lights of a patrol car off in the distance. I sat listening to the undulating hypnotic sound of the throbbing reel truck—that raspy old black panther's heart beating. Another night, another town. We roll again.

The rhythm of the road had a tranquilizing effect. Once the tent was down and reeled up on its truck, and the lot cleaned and the garbage bags lined up like duffel bags at a port of call, then, one by one, the grimy red trucks pulled out, evenly spaced like Rockettes peeling off in their dance step.

Down the back roads of America—the blue roads where the Corvettes and Porsches of the freeways seldom travel—where an old truck or an old bus looked not out of place beside a farm tractor or a Model A truck. America's real roads of the people were the blue roads.

16

That rolling down the road eventually took us somewhere. I wish it were home. But there was no home now, only the bus…and Curtis.

I had come too close to ruining our precious relationship. I blamed him. I turned away from him now when he tried to console me. I piled up guilts like Neena with the runs. I had hurt Curtis. I prayed, but the fear lingered on. I knew that from here on, with all my disquieting fears, there would be more trouble for me down the road. I was a ship breaking up in a storm. I was feeling ill. Thanks to running Pie Car and being around food all the time, I must have gained thirty more pounds.

Most of all was the frustration of not being able to do a good job. I was running Pie Car when I never had a concession before in my life. I had always worked in an office, doing books, typing, filing and accounting. Curtis was a teacher and a business administrator. Everyone on the show was doing the wrong job. Tom, the candy butcher, had been put on advance when he might have been better suited for doing Day-of-Show.

Advance was one of the show's biggest headaches. Several people could have handled it—Bob Seaton, for instance, but the advance people had to stay a week ahead of the show. Bob was needed more with the show. He was our only magician.

Even Curtis and I could have probably done Advance well, if we didn't have to be with the show. But who would run the office, or for that matter, run silly old Pie Car? Why couldn't Carmen carry short order food for the workmen in the concession wagon? Little Billy could sell pies, pop and candy as well as I could. Sure! I could easily be replaced by a four year old who knew the difference between a nickel and a quarter.

However, I think the main reason I entertained the idea of doing advance was that I might get to clown, to wear whiteface makeup and baggy pants that would hide my fat. I couldn't bring myself to do clown on the lot. It wasn't that I was a bad clown. It was that I "knew" they didn't want me any more.

Not being wanted was the story of my life. I guess I thought the circus world would absorb me like a giant squid sucking in a school of small fish. I really wanted so badly to be "circus." I wanted to stick it out, to make it through the entire season, to show up next year and never be First o' May again. I tried to think, but all I heard was the oompah circus music—the Sousaphone, the trumpets, the high, squeaking fife. Oompah! Oompah! This is my world now.

I busied myself the rest of the day cutting out Billy's new costume and frying chicken for the men. That night, as we traveled down the freeway, the bus was running so smoothly that I fell asleep.

I dreamed we were driving down the same road when Curtis himself fell asleep at the wheel. Then there was a little white poodle licking me in the face, trying to waken me, but we were both sound asleep and the bus continued on down the road as straight as if it were on automatic pilot. It came to a stop near a gas station and we woke up when the attendants put it up on the rack.

Suddenly, the bus lurched as Curtis hit an uneven patch of asphalt. I woke up, my heart pounding, my mouth dry. But Curtis was safe, just terribly tired. It was a confusing dream that left me feeling guilty for having fallen off to sleep when Curtis was dangerously tired. I made it a point each night to keep talking to him so he would stay awake.

We made it to the next town, but as we pulled off the road onto an asphalt shopping center, we knew the whole show would be out of sorts. They hated to set up on asphalt. After the stakes were pulled back up, all the holes had to be plugged by hand.

There was no business for Pie Car again. I was sabotaged by Seven-Eleven. There wouldn't be any business tomorrow either. They had an Alpha Beta to shop in. With my nose out of joint, I entertained the idea of just going back to sleep for the rest of the day. It was a ridiculous hour to be up. I looked out the window. The sun was barely lighting up the lot. The chiefs of war stood dressed in battle array of ragged cut-offs and torn levis. Instead of spear in hand, Bryan clutched a can of beer. Not even my beer! He had bought his own six-pack!

The men bent over and stooped to the ground. They formed their strategy for the day. The tent would go there, the sideshow over there. The advancing army of patrons would be expected that night, armed with toy spears and daggers of sticky cotton candy.

That night, there was no sponsor again. We were on a mall. The fire marshal had been out, raising hell, making Red put up more "NO SMOKING" signs. All the signs in the world wouldn't do any good. It was me catching the lighted cigarettes at the door and patrolling the crowd before the show began that did it. People ignored signs, but they couldn't ignore me.

Some big shot with the mall came over and complained about Neena's pee. I think Ron tried to tell him it was only water, but the guy didn't buy it. He should have asked the man how you diaper a two-ton elephant.

We all hated malls. Muddy fields were terrible, but nice clean asphalt malls were worse. Even though we had a hundred eighty mile hop that night to the next stand, Ron and Chris had to remain behind long enough to caulk up every damn hole in their precious asphalt.

I was in a bad mood, too. I had trouble on the midway. This weasely little thick-accented guy came up to me at the door, griping. "I'm going to call the cops on you! My kids went in there and never came out!"

"What in the hell do you think we are—Gypsies?" I mouthed back. "We don't steal kids. They probably split after the first show and are wandering around the mall having a good time with their friends. We run everybody out after the first show."

"No, they have to be in there!" He screamed hysterically. That was all I needed—a space case from One Step Beyond.

"Quit bugging me, Buster!" I said, getting hot. "No one threatens to call the cops on me without a damned good reason!" I snarled at him. I couldn't leave the door to get help. I yelled at Red, but he was busy with his midway spiel.

With a lot of gestures and yelling on my part, I finally got his attention and directed the irate father over toward him.

Red simply told him to go in and find his kids, even though they couldn't possibly still be in the tent. We had already had the blow-off for the first show and everyone had cleared out. That was what made this job so frustrating. Red was the manager and could let the man go in to avoid trouble. But if I did the same, I would be failing my responsibility.

It was my job to keep gatecrashers out. It was Curtis's job to handle the sponsors and it was Sandy's responsibility to see that the arrows were put up that guided us safely to the next lot.'

That night, Sandy stuck her head in the door and said, "Ninety-nine coloring books." She had sold more than the other three people combined.

"Directions?" she monotoned.

"This one's a piece of cake, Sandy," Curtis said. "I used to live in Milpitas."

"Oh, yeah, like you used to live in Modesto, right?"

"Sandy, just take Calaveras Boulevard. Go to the left to Main Street. Turn right. It couldn't be simpler."

We pulled out of Vacaville. Milpitas was a fairly long run, but all freeway. It should be easy. Then, going by the old Livermore turn-off, we saw a sign—CALAVERAS ROAD. It was a little winding back road through the mountains, past Calaveras Dam and, if not closed by rockslides, turned into Calaveras Boulevard—on the other end!

"Oops!" Curtis said. "I forgot about *that* sign. You don't think Sandy's down that road doing arrows, do you?" He sped by the Calaveras Road turnoff.

"Nobody in their right mind would try to get to Milpitas that way, unless they just wanted to get lost up a mountain road with no water, no phone, no service station—with a high pass to cross, narrow winding road and…"

But before we could think about the awesomeness of Sandy leading the circus over Calaveras Road, we had cruised through the wide mountain pass on the freeway, dropped quickly down the other side and soon saw the Milpitas turnoff sign that said, CALAVERAS BOULEVARD. As we crossed the overpass, we saw Sandy hurrying along the road on foot, doing arrows.

"I wonder why Sandy is so late doing arrows?"

Curtis looked at me. I looked at him. "Good God! You don't think she marked the wrong turnoff back there at the Calaveras Dam road, do you?"

Before he could answer me, Peewee passed us, missed the arrows and slid through a stoplight with his van. We made the turn smoothly and found the lot. Sandy was right behind us with her usual tornado scowl.

"I thought you knew this area when I asked you where we turned off, Curtis."

"I do know this area. I used to live here," he said, refusing to get ruffled. "I told you to turn at Calaveras Boulevard when you got to Milpitas."

"You *didn't* tell me there were two Calaverases," she said angrily. "I should have known—Modesto—two Hatch roads."

Peewee pulled in behind us. Carmen's concession wagon was pulled by the sleeper bus with all the boys in it, but Carmen and Billy rode with Peewee in the van and were probably sound asleep.

If Sandy was a tornado, Peewee was a hurricane. "I lost my fuckin' license 'cause of you!" he swore. "Where'n the hell were the arrows?"

Sandy blustered. "I took a wrong turn, man. I just got here."

Peewee went wild. He lashed out at her, striking a blow against her chest. Quickly, Curtis stepped between them, saying, "You can't hit her!"

"He's high," someone said as men poured out of the sleeper to see what was going on. "Let him go." Peewee ran off into the darkened night, a wild, frightened look across his face that I will never forget.

Sandy was shaking with anger. "I don't do it often," she said, rubbing the bruise on her chest, "but I'll get him fired. I'll tell my father."

But Peewee didn't get fired. By the next morning it had all blown over. It drove home how much everyone on the show depended on each other. Sandy depended on Curtis for directions. The whole show depended on her for arrows, so even when spaced out on "uppers" to stay awake on the long road, they could still find the lot. Even I depended on the circus's support of Pie Car. If business didn't pick up, I'd have to close down. They just didn't understand. I wasn't on salary. All I was getting was my profit from selling them food. If they didn't eat from Pie Car, I didn't make any money. And if I didn't make any money, I couldn't stay with the show.

Milpitas was supposed to be a red-letter stand. John had fussed for months about Milpitas because it was being booked by an old friend of his who promised it to be a good one. I had heard that before—in Arizona. One thing for sure—whoever chose the lot to set the tent up on must have hated Big John. The Fire Marshall ordered it plowed up the day before we arrived. Granted, high grass had to go, but newly plowed ground was murder on all of us, especially the patrons.

People began arriving. Before they could cross the field from where the cars were parked, high heels had already speared gobs of mud—so much that the women could hardly lift their feet.

But the show went well. We had several celebrity guests, among them, one performer from Carson and Barnes Circus. After the show, people stood around visiting for a long time. Even though Milpitas was on the fringe of a city, it had small town intimacy. One lady approached me and said, "I want to thank you. I enjoyed the circus tremendously."

In three months, she was the first person who had ever said thank you.

It took Curtis a long time to close office. He was unusually tired. We'd been having several long hops between stands and he was having to get up earlier and earlier each morning.

I had fallen asleep when he knocked on the bus door. I woke up and let him in, but I was so sleepy I did little more than nod and crawl back in bed. Then I remembered he hadn't eaten much earlier.

"Are you hungry?" He smiled so I crawled out again and fixed us a quick bite.

After he'd eaten, he started up the motor and prepared to move on. We pulled across the field to the garbage cans. Usually, I walked the garbage bag across before he got there, but after having gotten the bus bogged down in the mud earlier in the day and having to be pulled out by faithful Neena, I didn't relish plodding through the clods.

We heard the trucks start up. After the reel truck passed us, we pulled out on the road. I noticed Curtis hadn't brought his typewriter back from the office as he usually did each night, but it was just as safe in the office as it was in the bus.

The next day, we had a rare two-day stand. For the rest of the show, that meant a bit of relaxation—the only time off they got. But for me, I had a show to run on paper. Every extra minute I had free, I worked on the audit sheets. We were both very tired. Neither of us had gotten more than three hours sleep the night before. I was near to a breaking point myself and Curtis looked awful.

Big John stayed in a motel at night and bumbled around the lot by day, griping and groaning. It was an extra strain to have him on the show, but he had come up to replace Red. Though it was something of a mystery, Red suddenly had to fly down to San Diego on business, but he was expected back today. It must have been very important for John to have taken over in his stead. I'd be glad to see Red back. Then John could go home.

I was astonished when John finally spoke to me. He hadn't said two words to me since I was hired. I figured I should count my blessings. After all, I had been a real disappointment to the Strongs. It just hadn't worked, hiring someone who didn't know anything about circus life.

"Mrs. Erickson," he said, not smiling. "Have you seen the side show?"

I fell in like a pig in a mudhole.

"A lady just fainted in there."

"Oh?" I said, genuinely concerned. Then I got the message. That was part of his spiel. He was putting me on. He was practicing a new pitch to get people into the sideshow.

"Ladies and gentlemen, the oddities you will see are so amazing, a lady just fainted in there!"

After it sunk in, I felt more alone than ever. He didn't really know I existed. Bob Seaton was the only friendly face on the show. He didn't ever blame me when I got things all bawled up. Sometimes I think he had been appointed goodwill ambassador to the Ericksons. Without him smoothing things over, we couldn't have made it as far down the road as we did.

But later that morning, he was bearer of sad news. "Is this yours?" He held up a battered typewriter case.

"What happened to it? It looks like an elephant sat on it."

"I thought I left it in the office," Curtis said. "Now I remember I had it in my hand the other night when we left Milpitas. It was late, I was tired and I set it down when you handed me the garbage."

"You didn't pick it up?"

"I didn't pick it up," he said quietly.

"What happened to it, Bob?"

"Neena's van ran over it." He handed Curtis what was left of his portable electric typewriter.

"Sorry."

"An elephant did sit on it," Curtis moaned. "Just my luck."

Curtis took it well. What could he do? He wasn't the kind that cried. So I cried for him. "Oh, Curtis, what next?"

However, despite the mounting momentary personal tragedies, there were those moments when the circus life was so charming, especially the people who showed up to see it.

There were all kinds of ruses to see the show free, but the lemon lady was unique.

"I always bring lemons for the circus people," she said. She was fiftyish, pasty with gray-streaked hair. "I have lemons the size of oranges and oranges as big as grape-fruit and—"

"Do you have a ticket?"

"No, but see—I have all these lemons, except the rain this year—you know, but every year I bring them lemons." She didn't have anything in her hand, not even a pocketbook.

I turned aside to gather in more tickets while she continued her eulogy to her lemons. Her voice faded off as the circus music began. Then, the last I saw of the lemon lady, she went off in the direction of her lemon orchard, but didn't buy a ticket to the show.

17

We had a horrible date at Scotts Valley. The thing about Scotts Valley was that it was just the hole in the dam. The flood of people were all upstream.

The real population was about three miles up the narrow canyon at Felton.

We knew. Curtis had attended college at Bethany in Scotts Valley and I grew up just over the hill. But this time, we kept our mouths shut.

The show died at Scotts Valley because no one had papered Felton, or any of the other little towns along the highway.

I had some old posters from several towns back. I blotted over them with a felt pen. It was already noon when I got the makeshift posters ready. People would be getting out of church. They would go to Safeway in Felton, get some groceries and look for something to do on a nice spring day. They could be going to the circus if only they had known about it.

But I hadn't gotten the posters up in time. Too few people saw them. The performers had a hard time playing to an empty house. Maybe that's why Sherry and Curtis Cainian were all of a sudden so friendly. Maybe we all needed some reassurance now.

After the show, we dropped in at Denny's to eat. Sherry and Curtis Cainian hailed us over to their booth. I blossomed into smiles. Was this to be a break-through with the show people? If there was any caste system on our show, it would be the Cainians in top echelon.

Sherry's bleached hair stood out in that whole roomful of people, as well as her heavily made-up face and low cut blouse. Sherry always looked "on stage." Curtis Cainian, as usual, was quiet, shy, not quick to make any gesture of acknowledgement. He was dressed modestly in casual clothes. I was used to seeing him in red satin body suits. He patted Sherry's arm as we talked, saying little himself, being content to listen, to share and just smile his friendly, broken-nosed smile.

Sherry spoke slowly, giving deep thought to every word. She had worked for Franzen Brothers Circus before coming to Big John Strong's show.

"I was working horses when I heard Big John wanted an assistant for his jug-gler." She smiled at Curtis Cainian and he returned her affection adoringly.

He spoke up, still holding her hand. "I had tried out for juggling and auditioned at Ringling's. They said they liked my act, then they handed me a broom and a shovel."

"Big John brought us together," she said softly. "Curtis didn't know the assistant John had sent for was a girl—me." She giggled nervously.

So John also played cupid. He made a big thing about hiring only couples. This was a family circus. It was good for the show.

I was good for the show too. The work I was doing was vital. I was preparing all the receipts for the auditors. Then, when I had finished all the entries for the day, I had Billy's clown costume to finish. My hands were numb and pinpricked. Curtis had volunteered to help, but the worst part was trying to thread a needle. I had given up sewing years ago when my eyesight changed. Now, I had to have someone else do all the threading. Poor dear Curtis. I couldn't do anything any more without his patient aid.

I loved him more and more each day. This experience of our being with the circus only strengthened our personal relationship. We might appear like old fogies to the kids on the show, but in reality, we were ardent lovers, best of friends—pals. I knew couples who couldn't stand to sleep in the same room much less the same bed, or those who had to have king-sized beds. We always joked we could sleep on an ironing board, the way we entwined together each night like Rodin's lovers.

The least of our problems was the small space we were confined to. The interior of our bus was twenty-two feet long, but our livable space was something more like twelve feet long and two feet wide. The roof was less than six feet high. Curtis was six foot two!

He walked around all bent over, rotating back and forth from the dog's chair to the bed. We sort of melted ourselves around the bus. If Curtis got up, so did the dog and they exchanged places. Basically, there were only three spaces for the three of us.

We had tried to bathe in a bucket, but both of us were larger than our washtub. All we could do was stand in it and pour water down ourselves.

I had planned to bathe and wash my hair at Monterey. Playing fairgrounds, we usually expected to have electricity. That meant getting caught up on a lot of things, including showers.

Of course, nothing happened as I expected. We got in late, the gate was closed, we had to sleep on the street till dawn, still dirty. O'Flaherty, the gate man, was late to open the next morning. Red looked like he could cry any minute. We had three shows today to do and an all night run ahead. Advance had screwed us up again. Daryl threatened to quit so he was promoted to Advance.

"Advance is a lot of work if done right," Curtis explained to me. "But, a pitfall for some. Advance people stay in motels and have expense accounts. They also get Sundays off. But they aren't under immediate supervision, so it's easy to get in the habit of sleeping till noon. Advance's nice, but it's not the same as being with the show."

"How do you figure?"

"Because Advance people are always trying to get reassigned back to the show. Jamie had been promised his own lion act if he would do Advance for a year."

When we got to Scotts Valley, we found that Jamie had dropped three hundred dollars advance money in a Monterey massage parlor. The sponsor had to put up the necessary money for the show until Big John could straighten it out.

The posters hadn't been put up anywhere. Day after day all we heard was complaints about "the Advance." We were dying by stages because no one could be found who could go ahead and really electrify a town with the message, "The Circus is coming!"

I remembered when we started out, one sponsor said, "If only you could play near a military base on payday." Service men were notoriously broke near payday. We were a stone's throw from Fort Ord, one of the largest army posts in the United States. Not only were there no posters up, but we were playing here on the twenty-sixth of the month. The whole base was broke. They would've loved to go to a circus but they were just a few years too old for the free kids' passes.

I sighed as I fried chicken for the long "dukie run." I wondered at that funny expression. I knew a "dukie run" meant a long night with no chance to get a hot meal. It was traditional for the men to take a box lunch with them as they hit the road. But someone had once told me that the name originated from the fact that the first cook tent—I guess with Barnum and Bailey—was called Hotel du Qual. Anyway, I was frying up enough chicken for them to munch on all night as they drove down the road.

The next town was dead, too. Big John walked around forlorn, mumbling "This was my best town."

I think the economic slump was hitting the middle class the hardest. The poor were already on welfare. They bought family tickets for their large families.

But young fathers who had recently been laid off and still had high mortgage payments and credit cards to pay off showed up at the ticket window with strained faces.

At least John was looking better. He was even talking to me—at least complaining, which was better than nothing at all. He did call me "dear" once. I almost passed out from shock. I walked around for hours with my head in the clouds. But at this last town, all he could do was mumble about the coloring books.

At least it wasn't my fault that the coloring books went astray. Sending supplies to the show was an art. They had to be sent by regular freight to save money, and a guess made how many days P.I.E. would take to deliver them.

Hopefully, the show would be somewhere near the right city when they arrived. P.I.E. (Pacific Intermountain Express) sent all the coloring books to Salinas, but they didn't arrive until we were headed back toward the San Joaquin valley. They were then sent back to Sacramento. We wouldn't even be near Stockton for two more days and we were running out of coloring books.

"Simple," I told Curtis. "Stop selling so many coloring books."

"Ha!" he said. "This circus is operating on those coloring books."

"Well, I wouldn't worry too much. Not many people are showing up for the circus or the coloring books."

That night, I interviewed a man and his wife for Advance. She had done Advance before and seemed to know what it was all about. I sent them to Red, who in turn, sent them to John. He was delighted. The man seemed mature and dependable.

"It sounds great," the man said as he reached in his pocket for a small bottle of pills.

"What's that?" John said, losing his smile.

"Don't worry. I had a little heart problem, but it's okay now."

John hum-hawed around, but he didn't hire him.

We dragged in late but no one seemed to miss us. The men were still getting the tent up. After break, we drove back through town. We had to get the alternator fixed on our bus. We drove the whole length of town but we only found two places that had been papered—two back fences, one at each end of town.

"We won't make 'nut' here," I said to Curtis. He smiled knowingly at me using Red's favorite expression. "Making nut" was an old, old circus term dating back to when the circus moved on wagons drawn by teams of horses. Circus was a risky business, especially for townspeople who supplied hay and horsemeat and vittles. The tradesmen often didn't get paid so they would take the nuts off the wheels of the circus wagons. For a show to at least "make nut" meant to take in enough that night to buy back their wheel nuts whether they made a profit or not.

We had a long way to go to "make nut" for this town. I had seen the permits in the office which cost two hundred and fifty dollars just for the one day on the lot. The donikers were ninety dollars, and then, fifteen for garbage.

I was really surprised when we packed them in both performances. We had wall-to-wall kids, a carpet of sticky little faces, all the way to the ring curbs.

Everything went well, except the donikers didn't show up in time for the show. The kids all had short holding tanks and I was besieged with requests—"Where's the toilet?" I shrugged and pointed first one way and then the other, but every time I lifted the flap of canvas, there was a little faucet behind it, peeing.

There must have been a lot of complaints, because when we hit the next town, the first thing I saw out front was two donikers on their own little two-wheeled trailer.

Behind the donikers was parked a van I had never seen before. Marian passed by and identified it.

"That's Bucky Steele and his elephants. He's with Bentley Brothers. They'll be playing Marysville when we're in Stockton."

"Wow! California's going to be circused to death this season. Great American's hot on our heels, and Circus Vargas is playing the cities." I said.

There was the unmistakable odor of elephants emitting from the van. "Bucky's leasing six of his elephants to Bentley Brothers. We all know him and since he's this close, he's paying us a visit. I want you to be sure and meet him, Terry. He's a great man."

Red knocked on the door. "Did you call Sacramento, Curtis?"

"Yes, and the coloring books will be in Stockton."

"Good," Red said cheerfully.

"Do we have six new elephants?"

"Oh, no, they're Bucky Steele's. He's a famous man," Red said in hallowed tones. "He's very kind. He's got no ego—everyone likes Bucky."

Red's code was hard work, dedication and humility. Someday, someone would say similar things about him. "He's a good man," they would testify. "He's got no ego."

But I didn't catch the warning. It would surface later. Red's philosophy was a two-edged sword.

18

That night we remained on the old lot because the next stand's fairgrounds wouldn't be open until morning. Red hated for us to be parked out on the street. I slept fitfully. I dreamed I was a clown and it was time for my production number. I wore clown makeup but I had put my heavy winter overcoat on over my costume. Then I did something weird. I put a doll named EGO on a chopping block and hacked her to pieces like Alice Cooper would have. Nobody laughed. It didn't make much sense. My problem was being sensitive about being fat. Sometimes kids on the door sadistically teased me.

What does it take to be a sadist? Maybe they have to start young. There was this one kid who came to the show. He must have had a fat mother himself and had already learned the fine art of torture.

I had to run him off the midway. He was creating a disturbance. At first, I didn't hear enough of what he was saying because of the general show noise on the midway. That is, until he addressed me directly.

"Are you with the side show?"

"No," I said, trying to ignore him. I continued taking tickets.

"You should be. You're fat enough."

I should have mouthed back. I could tell him I used to be a Fat Lady with the circus but I went to Weightwatchers and lost so much weight, I got fired. Of course, it wasn't true. Instead, I pulled my blouse down over my bulging "chocolate chip cookie" tummy and wished I could get sucked up in a tornado like Dorothy to Oz.

The same brat tried to crash the gate at the second show. Again, I ran him off. Later, when I went back to the safety of my bus, I had no sooner settled down, pulled off my tight clothes and slipped into a loose muu muu than I heard the midway loud-speaker blaring. Only it wasn't time for the blow-off spiel.

I looked out the window. The kid had turned on the bally platform mike.

I thought, Oh, no! I'll get in trouble for leaving the midway early. Red would hold me responsible for anything going wrong on the midway. I yelled at him, but I couldn't be heard over the roar of the generator truck.

"Come on in, folks," he yelled into the microphone. "See the Fat Lady. She weighs five hundred and sixty pounds!"

It wasn't true, I wanted to scream! I was a few hundred pounds short of it.

He had struck a nerve and he knew it. Now he was closing in for the kill!

There were plenty of times I thought of quitting, but other times when I felt intensely loyal to the circus. Sometimes I wanted to cry, not for myself, but for my little "mud show." Especially when there was a "paper house." I believed that no one else was aware of the fact, or for that matter, was in a position to know or to find out, but me. After the show, they would just shake their heads—Red, Jay and Chris—while counting what little money there was and not even be aware of what had gone wrong. I called it a "paper house." That night, there must have been a hundred adults who had gone in with free passes, taking up kid space, not buying popcorn or cotton candy—certainly not coloring books.

One family presented four "free" passes pinned together, which proved to me without a question of a doubt, that VIP family passes were being given out indiscriminately. Those VIP passes were all signed by Tom, the one who had fallen through the tent and been promoted to Advance.

I complained to Red that there was too much "paper" being distributed. Tom overheard. He came over toward us with justification written all over his face in advance. He knew those free passes served a twofold purpose—to remunerate for favors or partially pay for a service rendered, or to generate business.

"The radio station did it," he said, all prepared. He shot angry glances at me.

Later, I told Chris that I had complained to Red, but was overheard by Tom. She always seemed to be my defender but I could see by the frown on her face that she considered me way out of line to find fault with a fellow worker.

But I didn't worry too much what Tom thought of me, as long as I was doing my own job well. I ran a tight gate to compensate for the light "takes." I collected every iota, jot and tittle. I was so tough at the door, the next thing I would be doing was charging for the toddlers. If they could walk and talk, they needed a ticket.

Sometimes it was terribly lonely on the door. That's when I tried to strike up conversations before show time when people were waiting in line for the second show. I amused the patrons with my "elephant" stories about Neena. I was telling about her pulling stake in Bullhead City, when I was interrupted by a soft-spoken man in light blue pants. "Your elephant's loose," he said politely.

"My elephant is what?" I yelled as I trotted down toward where Neena usually was staked. He was right! No Neena!

"She's behind that van!" someone else yelled.

I looked behind the van. Neena was nosing around, looking for a sack of dog food to get into.

My elephant was loose!

I scooted for the main tent, breathlessly calling for Jay to fetch Neena back. I don't know how she did it, but sooner or later, I knew she would escape from that new chain.

And Seaton was billed as the show's escape artist! Move over, Seaton. Neena's upstaged you!

When I got back to the door, the patron I'd been telling elephant stories to was in stitches. I guess I was funnier than the clowns, trying to run after an elephant as fat as I was.

"I thought you didn't believe my elephant stories," I told her.

"I believe you," she chortled, tears running down her face.

The real show was in the "backyard," getting the show down the road, trying to keep Neena around to do her act, pulling trucks out of the mud, washing a slippery bear, watching little Billy growing up on the midway, stepping over drowsy old Sparky, watching tent up, tent down a thousand times and—waking up in a different place every day.

Flickering flame is conducive to continuous contemplation. In pre-dawn hours, I found that eloquent solitude I needed to write, to think, to probe my mind's depths.

Great literature has been born by candlelight. Shadows cast by my pen against the flickering, moving, warm reflection of light are inspiring, as if Greater Power guided it along.

Mood music, a sip of exotic liquor, the sound of surf slopping against gray cliffs, the occasional cry of a seagull—the beauty of complete silence in my reverent solitude.

There's a difference between being alone and feeling lonely. When one becomes friends with himself, he's never alone.

It had been a short day. We spent most of it chasing down those damn coloring books. When we got back to the lot from P.I.E., the first show was already over. We'd been able to skip it because it was a benefit performance for the impoverished who had been brought to McClellan Air Force Base in buses. The second show was discounted.

"This must be why we're not making any money," I said to Curtis as I took ticket stubs for a dollar twenty-five an adult ticket.

"Hey," he said, "this is the most profitable stand we've had yet. The Air Force paid John several thousand dollars for the privilege of giving this show to Sacramento's poor."

Peewee began taking the midway tent down early. It even looked like the big tent would be down in record time. Everyone seemed in a good mood except for Tina. We were parked close to the animal van and I could hear her cussing.

"You big dumb brute!" she screamed with epithets. Neena had shoved Tina against the wall of the van while Tina was trying to load up the goats. Neena wasn't dumb. She got tired of sharing her quarters with goats, ponies and dogs. Neena looked over at me and winked one pretty eye. She wasn't dumb at all, just animal.

Carmen finished early, too, and began playing with Billy. She had taught him to do a handstand. He held his body rigid as his mother swung him between her legs and then upright on the palm of her hand. They had it down good. Carmen would be grooming Billy for a life of circus, just as Sandy had been taught by John, years before. It was inconceivable that any circus baby would quit and go into any other field.

I wondered about Sandy and John Jr. inheriting their circus. Something seemed terribly wrong from headquarters on down. There were so many changes that needed to be made if the Big John Strong Circus was to survive. But it wasn't easy to make changes, at least not as long as Big John still had a hold of the reins. The whole show prided itself on doing things just as it had been done a hundred years before. But the show had to be mechanized. That meant decent safe equipment that wasn't wasting time by always breaking down. It meant trucks repaired, motors overhauled, wiring made safe. It also meant some efficient system in the office so that the books could be understood and one could know what the hell was going on with that archaic disaster.

"Why do they crank the tent wheel by hand?" I asked Curtis. "A small electric winch would do it."

"Because they're an 1869 circus, don't you know?" He didn't smile. "They've got to do it like 1869."

"I bet in 1869 they didn't have an Advance man like Jamie."

"If they did, someone would've lynched him by now," Curtis said. "John was hopping mad this morning. Jamie spent five hundred dollars on radio ads."

"On top of the thirty or forty VIP passes that came in?"

"Yeah."

"Does John know?"

"John knows."

19

Highway 49 was a roller coaster of asphalt, hairpin curves and narrowed lanes that had, for the most part, been washed away by last winter's rains. We covered some sixty miles of it between Plymouth and Sonora by pale moonlight.

We started out alone, ahead of all the others, but when we stopped for supplies at a Safeway, one by one, the other trucks caught up and passed us. Once we got back on the road again, we weren't slow despite the winding road. Soon we were passing Jay with his two horses in their van behind his pickup. Next, we caught up with the elephant van.

By this time, the road had narrowed. There was no way around the smoke-belching red van. For a long time we had to follow behind until Bryan took a turn-out and let traffic by. Bryan was brave to drive that van in the condition it was in. Truckers say there's no load worse than swinging beef. How about swinging elephant?

Ron said it really got hairy going down a winding mountain road when Neena would get nervous and begin her swaying rhythmic dance. The van would bounce up and down with the hills, twist and turn with the curves and do something of a diesel disco from Neena's swaying back and forth.

I sighed with relief when we finally passed the van. Curtis didn't want to use the brakes unnecessarily, but we were constantly in danger of landing the bus in the show office that shared space in the elephant van if Bryan applied his brakes too fast.

At the Sonora fairgrounds, we were rewarded for the rough trip over the mountain with all night electricity. I was so tired after all that bouncing around that despite unlimited and uninterrupted power, I couldn't type, much less sew. But in the morning, I got back to working on Billy's costume right after doing Pie Car. With Curtis's help, we finished and presented it to Carmen. Billy would be a real clown tonight.

I never knew when a real VIP in the circus world would come through the gate. At Sonora, we had two famous people—Bob Yerkes's mother and Doc Monte, an old time PR man and friend of Big John's. Mrs. Yerkes stopped to visit with me.

"How did Bob Yerkes get into the circus, Mrs. Yerkes?"

"He had broken into show business from Muscle Beach down in Southern California, but he went on to do movies and some TV. work."

"Your son is more known now for his religious views. Has he always been religious?"

"No," she said. "He got religion when he was already a circus performer. For a long time, he questioned whether he should give up show business because of it."

"Oh, that would have been a shame, Mrs. Yerkes. This way, he can reach so many people."

"I agree. Recently, he taped a full interview of his life for the 700 club."

I would have loved to talk on with this gentle, charming woman, but I got busy on the door and soon she was being greeted by other people on the show.

Later, Doc Monte came by. Instead of the regular door VIP ticket, he had a permanent, sealed-in-plastic pass afforded only to special, special friends of John. Doc had worked for over fifty years with John. He told of one time when Big John announced him in the audience.

"I want to present to you my very old friend of twenty-five years," John said.

"Make it fifty, John," Doc said.

Maybe he was off a few years, but then, the time had slipped by quite easily. Doc was 93, but he didn't look sixty-three. I would've dated him if he asked me (and if my husband approved).

Doc Monte had yet to retire. He handed me his business card. He was still operating as a public relations man. He had lots of stories to tell so I asked if we could come back and interview him. Come to think of it, I hope we can last long enough to get back.

Doc Monte walked away with a bounce in his step, a twinkle in his eye and probably plenty of money in his pocket.

From Sonora we had to make Auburn in one jump. Just before midnight, the others pulled out heading down Highway 108 to 99. The twisting and winding on Route 49 was too much for the big rigs. But the monotonous bump-de-bump of the torn-up, unrepaired Highway 99 was just as bad for us, and almost fifty miles longer. We stayed on 49. It would be easier for Curtis to stay awake on a winding road. Less than a mile out of town, the bus filled quickly with smoke.

"We're on fire!" I screamed.

Curtis pulled over on the shoulder. For miles and miles on Highway 49, there was no place to pull over—as if the roadbed itself was hewn out of stone—yet, we had been fortunate enough to break down right there where there was perhaps the only pull-out for miles.

The moon was nearly full. We could see outside to move around. I had a new battery in my table lamp. There were spare batteries for the flashlight. We had water, toilet and food. We wouldn't be missed until 9:00 A.M. tomorrow!

When the wire burnt out, the motor quit. It took some time to find the bad wire. But when Curtis touched it, my nose verified that was the one.

From the alternator through the firewall to the ignition switch, the wire had burnt completely. Curtis always said there was no fuse box. A fuse should have blown first. We could have been cremated!

I stood on the step shaking. My first thought had been to get Shadow out safely, along with myself. Curtis already had the hood open. At lease we carried a fire extinguisher, thanks to my son, Danny, who had made sure we had one when we left Houston.

Then I remembered the back of the bus was locked! If the front had been on fire, an explosive fire, the key couldn't be reached in the ignition, the handle to the door too close to the fire, the front in flames, the back door padlocked, my key on a ribbon somewhere in the litter of my desk, maybe too difficult to find in my hysterical panic, me too fat to crawl out or be dragged out a window, and worse yet—no time! Both Shadow and I would be dead in minutes—horrible, agonized death by fire!

When I calmed down and Curtis began systematically tracing all the wiring, I stepped out of the bus, walked a distance away and began praying:

Our Father. You have always been.
We speak your Holy Name with honor.
You who reside above the heavens,
Hear my prayer this very hour.
Beyond the stars you reside.
Your temple is another dimension.
Beyond the thought of mortal men,
Yet you are as close as my prayer.
I gaze up into the heavens.
The blue is lighter for the full moon.
The stars are closer, luminous
For the unlit countryside—

For the exquisite loveliness of a warm spring night.

Thank you, Father, for we've been spared.

We continue living, safe from harm.

How can Your will be done on earth?

When will Your Kingdom come?

Curtis had patched us up with old wire he found elsewhere in the bus. Once back on the road, we made it as far as Placerville. Then, pulling up a steep grade, our engine cut out again. Curtis was too tired to trace down the problem.

We set the alarm for 6:00 A.M. and crawled in our sleeping bag. We slept, exhausted.

In the morning when the alarm went off, Curtis took off on foot in search of a mechanic. It was only a fuel line connection that had come loose. By 8:30 A.M., we were on the road again, only twenty-six more miles to Auburn.

But the road was rough and winding and try as we could, we wouldn't be able to make Pie Car. We crossed rivers, climbed mountains, dropped off into valleys and yet, the road seemed to stretch longer and longer.

When we got to the end of the line, the Auburn fairgrounds, there was Neena placidly swaying back and forth in heavenly high grass. The men, of course, had eaten at Seven-Eleven and I was so tired, I just sat down and cried.

We tried to get some extra sleep in the afternoon. The mind is treacherous—unpredictable. I was dizzy from the changing emotions and complexities of thought. I dreamed we were somewhere, nowhere like anywhere I'd ever been. It seemed to be more a carnival setting than a circus, with a giant midway, but no donikers.

In the dream I was worried about Red eating. I had encouraged him to stop and eat at a small sidewalk restaurant. What was important now was, not what was said, but what was felt. In the end, he allowed me to feed him.

In spite of missing Pie Car in Auburn, it seemed we were closer than ever to being part of the show. I busied myself working the gate and keeping my own personal watch over Neena.

I knew what had happened when the dog food sack flew up in the air. Neena had picked her footlock again. The next steps were repetitious. First, I shoved children back away from her and cried out a warning. Then I trotted off to fetch Jay. He chained her up again and took what was left of the dog food sack away from her. She was eating it sack and all. Poor Neena! Foiled again!

Later on in the day, I watched her. She was, once more, hard at work on the lock. The chain was slack. She lifted her huge foot daintily and studied it with the end of her trunk. I wondered if she might have flexed her muscles like an athlete when they put the chain on her leg. Was the loop of heavy chain around her ankle now loose enough for her to slip out? It was certainly loose enough for her to jiggle it good. Evidently she had found that worked and that sometimes the latch would pop open. So much for errant elephant antics.

The "new" Advance men came by the show to pick up their paychecks. Daryl appeared, clean shaven, dapper in well-tailored slacks and a cool light shirt.

His blond hair had been styled by a local barber to show off to the best advantage every deep wave. At least he would be the best-dressed Advance man we'd ever had.

Tom, however, looked clownish without being funny. He had a two-day growth of beard, messy clothes, pants too short for his tall, slender frame and a small-brimmed Alpine hat on top of his dark hair. His beard being almost jet black in color made him look like the blackface hobo clown painted on the side of one of the trucks.

I asked about Jamie, the Advance man who had been two weeks ahead of the show for most of the season posting the advertisements and making all the arrangements for the show. Daryl was discreetly silent, but I knew he and Tom were basically candy butchers trying their best to fill in. There was still no effective advance.

One morning I looked out the window of the bus door to see four golden paws carrying a huge ball of sheep-like yellow-orange wool. That was Sparky. Shadow began whining, but before I could let him out on his chain to play, Bob ordered Sparky back in the sleeper bus parked next to us. Shadow tore up and down the bus dismantling everything and almost knocking me over. He acted like he was madly in love with Sparky.

Sparky could run loose. He was a gentle Labrador. Shadow had to remain on a heavy chain because he, although equally loveable, was nonetheless a Doberman Pinscher. It wasn't fair, especially when we played a nice green, grassy fairground.

The manager of the fairground had gotten salty about letting us in the gate early. It seemed the custodian was on vacation. However, Curtis, who was becoming more "circus" every day, gave him his best line of complimentary bullshit. It was a singular triumph. By seven-thirty, the big trucks were able to move inside the fairground. It also promised to be a hot day.

There were no showers. The others, clad usually in brief shorts during the daytime, were now dressed in even briefer shorts. Carmen wore flesh-colored terrycloth jogging shorts. The Rivera boy with the Mephistophelean beard had on his favorite indecently ragged cut-offs.

"X-rated!" I yelled across the midway.

The sponsor snickered.

"See those sticks from the popped balloons?" I gestured at some lying on the ground. "Guess what I use them for? Every time he comes through the gate with a cigarette dangling out of his mouth, I whack him one across the fanny. He's getting the message."

"How come you're so hard on that particular one?"

"I guess I like him."

I loved the sound of the midway in early evening. People talk in low murmurs standing in line, quietly asking how much longer—children whining to ride the elephant and—Red spieling his exotic myths, downright lies and excited ballyhoo come-on.

"See the Fat Lady, right on the inside, folks. Five hundred and sixty pounds of feminine beauty. See Jojo, the dog-faced boy. It's all here on the inside, folks."

Very few complained that it was only pictures of oddities. They went in one door and out the other for twenty-five cents, looking at a strange collection of pictures—three-legged men, fat, skinny, deformed people, the mule-faced woman, fur-faced men, bearded ladies, midgets and giants.

They weren't seeing ordinary pictures, but one of the finest collections of freak pictures in existence. The display covered the history of modern day freaks on the sideshow since the days of P.T. Barnum.

Art Weaver of Lakeside, California, put together his "Freak Pictures" and sold the display to Big John Strong. It was now part of the circus midway attractions. The other attraction was Jim picking his nose with an ice pick, eating a little ignited lighter fluid on a stick and managing to be in two places at once. It isn't easy to do your own barking or spieling.

Then there was Billy on the bally. He loved to ham it up on the midway, pratfalling, climbing on the rigging, parading around in clown face and Pierrot costume.

Mornings on the lot were particularly charming. After the tent was up there were myriad other chores. People drift by. There seems to be an organized gait. Everyone moved peacefully—not fast, nor slow—as if Neena's swaying set the tempo. Tina, clad only in a wildflower sarong, unloaded her animals from the van. She picked up the heavy mallet and drove tent spikes to make a rope barricade. From within the van, the blue-eyed dog continuously kept yapping.

The run to Weaverville that night was the longest yet, over one hundred and fifty miles. We stopped in Red Bluff for a brief rest. From there we drove westward toward the ocean through the lovely Redwoods as we followed the winding Trinity River. It was a dark night. I knew those mountains. I could envision the color of the deepening purple masses as they grew higher and higher—the many hues of river rock—the kind I had always said that someday I wanted for a fireplace.

There I was—thinking about a fireplace built of beautiful Trinity River rock and I didn't even have a home. My home was a drafty old school bus rolling down a winding mountain road. My neighbors were an elephant, a bear and a bunch of yapping dogs.

I was still dreaming of that lovely mountain home with the rock fireplace when I was awakened by the circus dogs yapping at townspeople who gathered to watch the circus tent go up.

Neena, fresh from her early morning bath, trumpeted a welcome and Billy banged on the bus door. It was Mother's Day. I still had some of the lovely red roses a lady had given me in Paradise, California. I shared them with Billy and told him Carmen would like them. I wondered if he had ever called Carmen "mother", or Peewee "father." That just wasn't circus.

Billy was a working clown now. He got paid three dollars a night for his part in the production number. At the end of the week, he got paid with all the rest of the men. This morning, he paid for his breakfast out of his own money.

20

We were playing much smaller towns, way out in the boonies—beautiful, sleepy little towns hidden in the hills, nestled in canyons with a backdrop of pine-covered mountains in all directions. Besides the conifers, were the red spruce, the ever-present tough manzanita, some elm and the giant sequoia.

The Trinity River snakes a winding path down from snow-capped mother mountains. The river's coarse sands hold on to their jewel box of multicolored rocks. Some are red from the iron, some green from copper, others glisten with bits of fool's gold—mica. Clear blue water mirrors clearer blue skies as the Trinity cuts a swift path through dark mountain gorges bathed in eternal shadows.

The air is crisp with pine scent and new grass. The sun is warm, but the breeze is sharp, cool and fragrant.

Arctic currents push bergs till they melt in northern California waters. River torrents rush down to the sea, returning the moisture, the rain, the melted snow to Mother sea.

Melted snow makes clear cool streams and soft water. I remembered the soft water too late after having dumped soap in the Big Boy at the Laundromat. I sat down before the machine as I waited for it to explode into a froth of white lather, spilling out the top and down the sides.

While I was waiting, I cased the joint. The environment was hostile. Half of the machines were inoperative. The Big Boy looked as if it would digest and swallow my laundry at any moment.

Apple Annie in grimy khaki pants and a baseball cap claimed the rest of the machines.

"These's mine and them's her'n," she said with an unmistakably hilly voice. She was smoking a brown cigarette that looked like a miniature cigar. I rather expected her to pull out a corncob pipe. Her face was rugged and browned from the sun. Her brow was wrinkled and there were deeper brown age spots under her eyes and on her neck. Several front teeth were missing. Her arms were muscled as if she swung an ax every day of her life.

Her friend, the possessor of all the remaining machines, was short, squatty and sniffly.

"Ah'm allergic to everything," she complained in a whiny voice, "even the allergy medicine the doctor gives me." Her hair fell down in her eyes, dry and stringy. She was so full-bosomed she looked like she'd topple forward any minute. The two townswomen whined back and forth the local gossip.

"Miz Collins had her operation," one said.

"Turned out okay, too," the other said. "She had a little boy."

"I thought she said it was a tumor."

"Cud a been—or maybe should a been. Her husband's been gone more'n a year."

Apple Annie sorted another load, matching mismatched socks together with at least the stripes nearly in color, until she got down to one purple and one green sock. She studied them for a moment, then quickly folded them together.

Bosom Betty sat down beside me and wiped her nose on a dirty T-shirt.

"You have an allergy?" I asked.

"No, this time I caught the flu and my nose won't quit running."

I got up quickly and moved across the room.

That night, we had a good gate and I had a dear sweet old Lion to help me take tickets. I met John Miller and his wife, Trudy, and their baby, Joy, who used to be with the Big John Strong show over eleven years ago. He said he was a Christian now.

"So's Big John," Trudy said. "Did you know that?"

I didn't answer, but we exchanged addresses and I said I would answer their letters. I had told so many people I would write to them, that if I ever settled down again, I would have to hire a secretary just to keep up with the mail.

Even on the road, I wrote quite a few letters. Sometimes I had electricity late at night if we were playing a fairground, but usually I was too tired to write by then. Curtis bought a converter but it could only be used if the spare battery was up, and tonight, it was down.

I had to depend mainly on candlelight. One candle wasn't very bright, but surprisingly adequate and cheerful.

I made up a pot of cocoa because it was so cold after the sun went down. The candle made it seem warmer with its flickering lively flame.

Some of my best work had been done by candlelight—one candle power. There is something so creative in the act itself, of writing by candlelight, as if I were able to turn the clock back a century—as if it were really 1869.

Jim interrupted my mindwandering with a knock at the door.

"Can I have another candy bar?" he said, like I was his mama and he had to have permission as well. He had already eaten two candy bars earlier in the day.

"You sure can," I said. I thought how young he was, how childlike when he was around me. Jim was one of the best jugglers and rola bola men I knew.

"Can I have two and pay you tomorrow?"

"Sure," I said, reaching for the tab sheet. Jim and Red were my best customers, even if it was on the cuff most of the time.

Curtis returned to the bus with his arms full of office entry books and dropped something on the table.

"This three year-old came up to the window with her mother," he said. "I started to tell the mother that the little girl didn't have to pay when the little girl handed me this." He showed me a piece of paper. "The mother whispered to me, 'She wants to pay.'"

I examined the green paper. It was a twenty. Across the top of the note, it said PLAYTOWN BANKER. NOT NEGOTIABLE. In the center was a picture of two happy children. Non-negotiable was too big a word for a three year old to understand. I smiled at Curtis. He'd remember such things for a long time.

The next day was warmer. Pink-cheeked children sat on the rail fence watching the tent go up. Old men stood knee deep in uncut hay, watching too.

"Hit it! Hit it!" chanted the men. Neena groaned and tugged to her knees as she dragged the heavy centerpole in place.

The oldest Rivera, now known as Muhammed, swaggered by, tentspike in hand, everlasting rotten cigarette in his mouth. When he wasn't candy butchering in the tent, they had him sitting outside on the sideshow bally platform, looking like a fakir. I explained to Red that it was pronounced fah-keer, which he seemed to appreciate. I guess Red hoped Muhammed would evolve into some kind of an act, but after a few times of just sitting there looking stupid, Muhammed retreated back into the big tent to his cotton candy. I laughed when I looked up the word *fakir* to get the correct pronunciation. It meant mendicant, a dervish, and in other words—bum.

Muhammed joined the other men as they went through the different stages of erecting the tent.

Ropes hung slack and canvas that had not been drawn taut swayed slightly in the wind. A week ago, we'd have been knee deep in loamy mud, but warm days had dried the ground into ridges and ruts and we were counting our blessings.

Men worked to finish Tent-up on empty stomachs, skipping Pie Car. They were two hours behind schedule. The reel truck had run out of gas and was forced to remain behind until morning at a gas station in the last town we played.

The Riveras worked silently, stretching ropes out, removing snarls in the lines, tightening guy lines.

Sparky sauntered from man to man, getting under foot, trying not to be in the way—being very much in the way like a true "auguste" clown.

The ocean fog lifted. Warm rays of sunlight pierced through the bone-chilling cold. A few days ago, the men worked nearly naked except for ragged cut-offs. Now, they shivered in heavy jackets. We would have four more cold coastal days before returning to the valley heat.

The voices of the men rang out sharp and clear as they tugged in unison on the main bowline. Now the canvas stood taut and trim, flags flying high.

Sparky dug another gopher hole and sat down beside it, tail wagging. Neena grazed contentedly in tall grass while Tina and Sherri stumbled almost nude over piles of saddle blankets.

The whole town came out to the show. For a week, McMinleyville had been made circus conscious. It had been circus week. Now that's the way Advance was supposed to be handled. Everyone in town was involved. Even the bank tellers dressed as clowns and wore red fright wigs.

Every store displayed ads. Every child had his free ticket. Adults had time to save back for their own tickets, or else, had obtained advance sales coupons by donating to the town's particular charity.

Despite a packed house for the first show and a comfortably full house for the second, the take at the gate was light. Advance had done such a good job, almost every kid in town got in free. There was a scarcity of VIP passes due to my hell-raising, but those that did come brought six non-paying adults with them.

When I'm working the door, I often have a moment's intimacy with the people. I feel close to them—involved. I had noticed this one woman waiting across the street for her children. We were running overtime due to a packed house. Red didn't like to begin the show until everyone was settled down in the tent. It was a losing battle because stragglers came in all the way to intermission.

"The show will run at least fifteen minutes overtime," I said, raising my voice so she could hear me. I studied her face. There were heavy harried lines of worry despite the friendly smile. She crossed the street toward me.

"Is there anything wrong?" I asked.

"I have to be sure to catch my daughter and her friend in this crowd."

"They all exit out one entrance. You can stand here beside me if you like."

She stood back away from me with her eye on the street. "I can see my daughter's pickup from here. She has my neighbor's child with her. I want to stop my daughter before she drops the child off at her home."

"Why?" I asked, sensing something terrible had happened.

"Her brother fell. He was biking. His head—he has a fractured skull."

"That's awful! Would you like to go in and find them?"

"No," she hesitated. "When they see me, they'll suspect something's wrong. They've waited all week to see the circus. It means so much to them. I want them to enjoy every minute of it first."

"How is the injured child?"

"We don't know. The parents took him into the Eureka hospital. They didn't want the little girl to be alone at their farmhouse," she said. "But I'll wait right here. I'll be sure to catch them."

Special, I thought. We were very special for all these kids. The whole town had waited for us to arrive. Had I become jaded so soon? Would I ever get to where I didn't care any more about each and every child? I must remember to greet each child, not just grab tickets. We were the most important people in their lives, at least for tonight only.

The boy that was hurt—I would never find out whether he recovered. We had to keep the show moving. Everyone had to work together. Children were waiting in the next town for their circus.

So many things were going wrong with the show. Some of the trouble might have been prevented if we only had a real mechanic who didn't have to juggle or do rola bola. A mechanic couldn't work the tent and work on the vehicles at the same time. It would be a real tragedy if all the children came but the circus didn't.

So far, there had been several times we almost lost the whole show, what with bad roads, breakdowns and missing Sandy's arrows.

Sandy took her arrows so seriously. We were beginning to understand why. Without them, the circus could become hopelessly lost. Those black arrows in the middle of the night guided our way.

"Arrows!" I would shout gleefully when they began appearing on signposts and telephone poles alongside the road.

"More arrows!" I called out. First there was the angle turn, then straight ahead. After that came one down, three to the left (or right). Another block and one down, two right. Another block and one right. Then there would be an explosion of arrows. Sometimes Sandy would exuberantly put five or six turn arrows up that seemed to scream out—"Don't miss the turn!!!!"

We couldn't ever blow a stand by not showing up. We were too important to all those children in all those towns. Some had never seen a circus or an elephant before.

21

Everything on the show was predictable, except when and what the guys would eat. Tonight, it was colder than a polar bear's arse with an Arctic wind spanking down on the bleak Northern California coastline.

I assumed Billy would be over for his nightly bowl of steaming hot chicken noodle soup, especially tonight. I was wrong. All I got was caffeine-happy Riveras.

I made a second pot of coffee. Even Jim came back for a second cup. He was driving tonight.

But I missed Billy. One Billy was worth three and a half Riveras. Coffee was thirty cents a cup, but Billy's noodles cost a dollar a bowl.

Slowly, our life was beginning to be as organized as the show. I could tell time by whatever act was on. I woke up each morning to the raspy purr of the reel truck. I dressed to the opening music in the evening. I went to bed at night to sounds of the tent being taken down.

Little disturbed the routine unless it was someone wanting something at the last minute when I was rushing to get on the door by 5:40 P.M... All it took was someone like Marian wanting soup and salad at the last minute.

No one else was giving me any trouble. At first, I had some friction with the Riveras, but I raised enough hell with them to keep some semblance of order the rest of the season. We now called Muhammed, "Prince." His act had failed to mature, but he still had that lovely pointed beard which set him apart from the others. He would put in his order at 8:30 P.M., when I entered the tent with volunteers to assist the magician, Bob Seaton.

They would help him into his strait jacket for the escape act. Then Prince would pick up his order during intermission. After the show, I could always expect Jim and the others to drop by for a cold drink before taking down the tent.

I had to rush to do my chores, whether making coffee, vacuuming the bus, typing or posting the receipts. I had little time before my electricity was cut off from the main generator. The plug was pulled when they moved the reel truck. From then on, I was on candlelight power until Curtis came and started up the bus. We pulled out every night around 11:30 P.M. if all went right.

The road to Laytonville was rough—half washed away by recent winter rains. Where giant redwood groves were, the road narrowed so much that I held my breath as diesels approached us from the opposite direction. We passed the sleeper bus. Its motor sounded threatening. If it blew up, how would all the workmen be transported at night and where would they sleep? Yet, no one was assigned to any preventative maintenance. Even though all the men were adults, no one took any initiative. It was as if they were all on vacation.

Some people vacation with cameras in hand, capturing human interest, catching people unaware, preserving on celluloid human-interest scenes. But I wasn't comfortable with a camera. I caught human-interest in my writing.

There was this one young girl with straight hair down to her waist, clothed in shapeless tunic of sackcloth and wearing a black sweater torn at the sleeves.

She walked up to Sam and bought a bird. The birds were made out of brightly colored bits of paper and had a whistle inside.

Sam reached out her hand for the coins and the girl dropped a small packet in Sam's hand.

"That'll more than pay for the bird," the girl said as she disappeared into the crowd.

Sam unfolded the packet. In it was a small amount of homegrown marijuana. We were in the marijuana capital of California and the local townspeople believed in a barter system.

Just before the show ended, a little girl about ten years old came up to me.

"Do you know what my favorite dream is?" she said.

"No," I smiled. I remembered I had dreams too when I was ten. She was chubby like I was at that age and there was a far off look in her eye.

"I want to grow up and join a circus."

"I ran away with the circus, only I had to wait until I was a grandma. That had been my dream too."

There was a certain camaraderie between our generations. We became two little girls sharing secrets, making plans.

Earlier, a grown woman dragging two dirty-faced children and a sullen husband said something of the same thing.

"I always wanted to join a circus but I can't travel," she whined. She walked past me with her husband dragging behind.

I ignored her but I wanted to say—if you can't travel, you can't be circus.

Maybe someday, the little girl would make it—like me, like Red, like Chris and Ron—like Jim.

I got a chance to catch Jim's act in its entirety. He was great, especially the clowning effect, the bizarre jacket with stripes and pants with huge checks.

"Jim Zychek, direct from Czechoslovakia," Red pitched. The closest Jim got to Czechoslovakia was on a world map. But whether he came from Michigan or Hoboken, Jim was a good juggler and a great comedy act.

He stumbled into the arena as if he were terribly nearsighted. Wearing oversized clodhopper boots, he climbed clumsily onto a table, then onto a board balanced on a cylinder.

Once on the rola bola, he was master of grace and balance. He revolved the ball with one finger and transferred it onto a mouthpiece. Then he juggled several items at once, all the time still balancing on the rola bola. He could pass his whole body through three hula-hoops or even jump rope. Meanwhile, Curtis Cainian was juggling five balls in the other ring.

That night it was a long winding road that seemed to be mostly downhill, back into the Sacramento valley where it was hot. I volunteered my fan to keep the amplifier from blowing up, but after one hour in the bus without it, I unvolunteered it. Curtis fetched the fan right back at the end of the show, which was very "uncircus" of us.

The next morning, we woke up in Roseville. Bob headed downtown on a Sunday morning to try to buy a fan to cool the amplifier. By 5 P.M., it would be sizzling. Today, I certainly wouldn't loan the fan out to cool the amplifiers or anything else but me. I let it run all day long in the bus.

All that fuss so we could "die" in Roseville.

"Die" we did. About eight families showed up for the first show and half of them had VIP passes. The second show wasn't any improvement. I yawned and came in early—so early that it was five minutes after show time.

After the show, Curtis came back to the bus. The windows were open and we could hear John and Red talking.

"...and Curtis comes dragging in here at noon," Big John said.

We had slept around the corner on a cool tree-lined street, but we arrived on the lot in time to do Pie Car. I was furious. But I didn't know we weren't the ones John was mad at. It was the day he had to fire Jamie.

Jamie came by for a cup of coffee and goodbye. I hugged him and asked him to write, but I feared I'd never see him again. He said he had worked out of Palmdale and trained cats for movies. I really liked Jamie. He was impossible not to like. That's why it hurt John so much to have to fire him.

The mail arrived with Big John. Most of it was for me. I got a letter from my friend Mac (Clark McDermott of the Cold Nose Five), commiserating with me for being on a mud show. I felt sorry for me, too. More, I felt sorry for the others on the show. They knock themselves out night after night, with little praise.

Before Jamie left, we talked about what he would do next.
"I guess I'll look around for a job as a cat handler," he said. "You know that's what I am."
I felt sorry for Jamie. An advance man is an advance man and a lion tamer is a lion tamer. "What happened to Cliff Vargas's beautiful white tigers?"
"They're not albinos, you know." He brightened up. Talking about something he knew a lot about cheered him. "All kittens have blue eyes when they're born, but those tigers keep their blue eyes."
"Where do they come from?"
"They're bred…mutations, you know. They're hard to work—a little crazy. It's the mutations."
"I thought they were lovely."
"Yeah, but a cockeyed cat who can't see very well—they're a little cross-eyed too—they can be sneaky."
I tried to imagine getting serious over a cross-eyed cat who bumped into things.
That was the last I saw of Jamie.

When the circus headed for Dixon, we went to Emeryville for more coloring books at P.I.E. We parked by the San Francisco bay. I sat staring at the water through the front windshield, hypnotized by the shimmering reflections of skyscrapers beyond. Cars passed down the freeway—a series of red dots like bleeps on an Atari game. Now and then, a tall truck bleeped by, decked out in greens, reds and oranges. It was now—moments like these—that I was hit with terrible melancholia, longing to be back where memories were—painful memories.
We slept undisturbed, lulled by the slap-slap-slap of gentle waves against the shoreline.
Next morning, I awakened as if I had heard the diesel circus trucks starting up. The only trucks were the ones plodding along the freeway.

We had been sent to Emeryville to get the coloring books. If we didn't make it to Dixon before 10:00 A.M., I lost Pie Car business for the day. To make matters worse, I had promised the men fried chicken. I had three raw chickens on my hands and maybe no Pie Car stand today.

Rays of light crept over the east shore mountain range. The tide slipped out, leaving the bay placid. The highway filled up with early morning commuters. I had needed the sleep, but more—needed time and solitude to think and write.

Curtis stirred and the bus rocked. He was silently beckoning me like Captain Ahab tied to the side of Moby Dick. He was disturbing me even though he didn't mean to. Anyway, soon it would be time to fetch the coloring books, so I put away my journal.

We found P.I.E. wihout any trouble. We had parked and slept almost directly across from it. By 7:30 A.M., we had loaded up the coloring books and had pulled back on the freeway. Curtis must have hit seventy miles per hour with the old school bus but we made Pie Car.

Later that day, I cooked the chicken.

"Rumor has it," Bob said, sniffing the air, "that you are cooking chicken."

He had me worried for a moment. But then they all liked chicken. We had done three things right today. It was cause for celebration. We got the coloring books, made Pie Car and I had fried chicken ready for tonight. It was going to be another "dukie run."

At the next town, the fog lifted, the sun came out and it became a pleasant clear blue-sky day. I fed the men, cleaned the bus up and made myself a brunch sandwich of liverwurst, onions and alfalfa sprouts on black bread.

Billy popped in and out again, wiggling a rubber dragon on the end of an elas-tic band.

"That the same dragon you had last night?"

"Yep. I got a nose too."

"I saw your big nose and glasses. That's a Groucho Marx," I said. "Where'd ya get your nose?"

"Jay," he said, handing me his empty bowl from the night before. Billy and his dragon exited. I finished the last delicious bite of my liverwurst and alfalfa sand-wich.

A few days before, he had a different prop. Jay had given it to him also. Jay, who read books, studied languages—a quiet, introspective man who loved his horses, solitude and children. It wasn't only Billy. When Jay was in the ring, he played directly to every kid in the audience. That's what it took to be great—loving and caring, like Mickey Rooney and Pinky Lee.

I was still awestruck every time I saw John's "kids" perform. That's what Big John called them—his kids. They were all so talented. Again, I wondered what I was doing with this circus. I may be the reigning queen of the Pie Car, but I had no act at all. It humbled me to be surrounded by so much talent. If only I could bring myself to do "clown."

Just then, Bob came by with a piece of good news. Bob Owen, who was Spiff, the clown, was coming back to the Big John Strong show as Advance man.

He and his partner, Dixie, were stilt-walking clowns.

That was the best news yet. We were leaving California. The show was headed east into Nevada, then Oregon and Washington—small towns, rural areas.

It was while playing Roseville that I first met Bob Owens (Spiff, the clown) and Little Dixie. Red introduced them to me. Later, they came on the midway in costume—the most colorful, gaudy, silly, happy clowns I'd ever seen. In or out of costume, they were delightful, which was a big change from the kind of clowns we had on the show.

I wanted to be a happy clown like Dixie, not sad like Sam or dull like BJ. My idea of my own clown ensemble was good, because Dixie had a similar get-up. Her red fright wig was pigtailed with wire so the pigtails stood straight out at right angles. Her costume was a little girl's dress in wild colors and patterns.

After their walkaround in the tent, they exited out the back door and stilt-walked across the lot. For once Sparky came alive. As usual, he was playing dead on the midway, a trick we hadn't needed to teach him. He was draped casually over a pile of folded sidewalls where everyone had to step around him.

When he saw the stiltwalkers, he bolted upright and began barking furiously.

I ran to get Peewee.

"You know what's the matter with Sparky?"

Peewee held him back, but he barked all the louder. "You forgot to introduce him to Spiff and Little Dixie."

Peewee grabbed the wool of Sparky's neck until his fingers found a hidden collar. Tugging him along, Peewee headed in the direction of Spiff's bus.

A few minutes later, the barking stopped abruptly. Obviously, they had been properly introduced.

22

Big John said we would be in Wyoming around the first of August. Sometimes, when I realized how much land we were covering, it became staggering. There were times when I longed to remain on firm ground instead of bouncing down the asphalt every night. Once in a while, I weakened and thought of living in port. I had left our address with a realtor in Felton, down near Santa Cruz. We got back a brochure advertising their special gems.

There was a listing in Whalebone Gulch off Bear Creek road. It was gently referred to as a Lost Dutchman's cabin with towering redwoods standing sentry, awaiting his return. The well (at least there was water) was recently replaced. The cabin needed lots of tender loving care but would make a perfect retreat. The land, however, was very steep and heavily wooded with redwood.

It sounded great except I knew where Bear Creek was. It was straight up and down, no roads into the land and trees too thick to make a road. It would be great if we packed in by mule. There was water but no plumbing, no toilet, no bath—probably no roof either. But then, we could enjoy the evening stars.

I must have had stars in my eyes because it was listed at only $34,000, and that was the lowest piece of land that broker had. The cabin was about 18 by 22 feet even though the lot was quite large. Anything that resembled a livable house was in a much higher price bracket.

I looked at my cheerful little bus, all paid for, with a new motor and transmission, gas paid, electricity furnished (sometimes), pot to pee in and window to throw it out of. All I had to do was serve a bunch of men coffee and candy bars all day.

We had a long road ahead of us and a lot of miles back. We would still see some magnificent country. I sat watching cars go by, the beautiful snowcapped Sierras in the background with Mt. Rose towering over the valley.

God's green earth was gorgeous. I wanted to check out my inheritance carefully.

I often wondered about religion with circus people and how they felt about it. Sometimes I thought I was in a lifeboat with a bunch of strangers. In one town, I met a lady who taught John's kids in Sunday school. So The Strongs, for that matter, had been exposed to religion. In fact, Curtis said that John goes to church every Sunday when he's home.

In Gardnerville, Willie Nelson's manager came in on a VIP pass. He looked enough like John to be a brother. I asked him for his address so I could send him a questionnaire about John but he disappeared into the crowd.

Tonight, It was a good crowd with both shows a packed house. The first show ran overtime and I had difficulty getting the tent cleared for the second show. Neena was kept busy with the rides. John yelled at me to hurry and open the gate. I had paused for a minute to finish a sentence with someone at the gate I was entertaining. John didn't have to get so all fired snippity about it, even if he did own the show.

That night, Big John was the announcer. Dressed immaculately in a medium blue tailored suit that showed off his beautiful white hair, John began his speech. I had heard it all before. Only the name of the town and the sponsor had changed.

The sponsor gave a speech, too. She was the head cheese in this town, probably running for office. The show didn't start until well after 8:30 P.M., which made the last show run a half hour late. We were all so progressively tired, that one half hour made all the difference in the world, especially with the longest single run yet ahead of us that night.

It was something of a jumping off point. Gardnerville was the closest to California we would be for months. John drove south to Yucaipa. The show moved east to Laytonville. Red came in with a new route sheet in his hand. "Good news," he announced. "There's an end to all these one night stands. We play two days in one place in Wyoming."

I had a sick feeling as I watched the men load up. They seemed to drag. Instead of fifteen minutes to midnight, our usual moving out time, it was almost one in the morning before we passed through Carson City. I don't know whether we were first, last or in the middle, but the only circus rig we passed was Red driving the reel truck, heavily loaded with the tent. He seemed to be lugging it on the hills, as if the canvas had grown heavier. It was hard to decide which was the most tired, the truck or Red.

The turnoff road wound quietly through barren black hills. Every ten minutes or so a car would pass us going the other way, but for the most part we were alone on the dry bleak desert after we zoomed past the reel truck in our hot rod "Camaro" bus. This time, I shared no glee with Curtis. I would have rather remained behind Red to know that he was safe.

My mind drifted back. It was years before and I was tailing my ex-husband home. I was driving the white Cadillac and he was in the diesel cab with the trailer behind. He was weaving from side to side and I knew he was going to sleep. I jammed the horn down as hard as I could. The sound of the horn reverberated against the canyon wall. On the other side was a steep drop off, straight down. I knew I had jarred him awake because he jerked the wheel hard. The truck rocked back and forth and settled for the middle of the road. He hung on to that white line for a moment, then regained his correct driving position on his side of the road.

One consolation—if Red drifted off to sleep and off the road, he would scrape up a few tumbleweeds and come to rest in a mound of desert sand. Nevertheless, I was worried.

We saw yellow emergency blinkers on the left side of the road up ahead. A man was flagging us down. We couldn't leave him stranded out like this, but a wave of apprehension made me tug firmly at Shadow's collar. I was ready to release him if Anything went wrong. But the man seemed gentle enough. He had left his wife and two children in the car and was going for mechanical help.

When we stopped at the junction to drop the man off, Red passed us. He had missed the turnoff and was headed for Fallon. I checked the map. It was the longer way but he could get to Lovelock sooner or later.

It figured that we would be the first ones on the lot. Curtis and I were night people. We thrived on the late hours. When everyone else was dead tired, we were just coming into our zenith.

We turned off one street too soon, so Sherry and Curtis Cainian passed us by. Technically, they'd be the first ones to the lot, but we were ahead of the pack. Quite a difference from how we started out, crawling up anthills in granny gear, always the last to pull in at night.

The morning in Lovelock was warm and quiet. We could still see white-capped mountains on the distant horizon. I set up for Pie Car and Curtis made his initial visit to his "office" in Neena's van.

He returned with a disgusted look on his face. "You should see the office. I swear it looks as if it had turned completely upside down. You know the cabinet? It's all over the office."

I sympathized with him. I knew how hard he'd been trying to keep order in that impossibly disorderly place. For the first time, I was glad the receipts were safe here in the bus, even if they were always in my way.

"I've got to put up frames to hold everything in place. It's an awful mess."

"What do you think happened?"

"Bryan was driving," Curtis said. "He was overtired." Curtis paused for a moment before deciding to share with me what he had come to know from the lot show gossip. "You know Tina made him quit drinking. He was used to it. Bryan stopped once in the night and ran around out in the field to wake up. But nothing can replace having enough sleep. These long hops after days of tent up and tent down are getting to all of us. The boys badly need rest."

"But what happened to the van?"

"Bryan said one minute he was okay and the next, he was on the shoulder, fighting to get the van right side up again."

Oh my God, I thought! It must have been like when Curtis made that horrible left turn in Colusa and the refrigerator flew open, only worse. At least we didn't have two tons of elephant in the back.

"They shouldn't have taken his beer away from him. Bryan beered out in the afternoon and slept. Now he's a bundle of nerves. He doesn't rest in the afternoon without the gentle tranquillizing effect of the beer, and consequently he's really too tired to drive."

"Maybe so," Curtis said, "but you know what's the really weird part of it all?"

"What?"

"I couldn't sleep last night," he said. Curtis always slept soundly. "I don't know if it's ESP or sixth sense or what, but I knew something was wrong."

Red interrupted us, looking for coffee. Curtis told him about feeling some ill omen. Red listened.

After he left, I said, "He heard you, all right. Circus people believe in that stuff. Remember what Mac said about peacock feathers and a camel-backed trunk? Wearing yellow's another superstition. I think Lillian Leitzel was wearing yellow when she fell."

"I usually keep my mouth shut about such things."

"Just the same, we could've lost the show last night, as well as Bryan and Neena."

"That'd do it."

After that night's show, I was stopped by two well-dressed women at the end of the midway.

"Why can't you play two days?"

"It isn't practical."

"But some miss the show."

She was one of those agitators. "It's too bad you have to go to all that work for one night," she cooed.

"We couldn't fill the seats for the second show. What would we do for a second day?"

"It's a shame for you to have to go to all that effort for only one day." She said it as if it were sinful for us to work our asses off for the show. I thought of the men working together, singing Irish chanties as they tugged the canvas. The more tired they were, the bawdier and more joyful were the songs. It became a cadence. It was their attack against fatigue. It wasn't the work. It was not getting enough rest with it.

I picked up on her vibes. I was just as hostile. She quickly moved away and began visiting with some friends. Then another girl approached me.

"Hi, I'm Joanie," she said cheerfully.

We visited a long time. I told her all about our little circus. I got so involved I didn't notice the time slipping by. When I got back to the bus, I tried to make coffee, but the damned breaker box went out four times just making one batch of coffee. I was too tired to put up with it. We badly needed a new breaker box.

It's a long, long road to Winnemucca. This time Curtis couldn't make it. I took the wheel. I was fighting sleep too, but my specialty had always been night driving. We passed the elephant van. This time, Bryan pulled over himself when he started to fade.

It was a survival story from the beginning—a battle between men and natural forces. The odds were completely against Curtis and me making the season all the way to the end. But, for that matter, the odds were even against the show itself making it through the season.

It was a saga of human endurance, filled with danger, excitement and hopeless frustration. I was writing a log. No, this wasn't a log of a business trying to survive. It was a report of an accident waiting to happen. This circus was courting disaster, flirting with death—dealing against impossible odds. Ten dozen new possibilities had surfaced to kill the show.

One would have to travel with the show like we did, to understand that the tented circus was a rolling financial disaster. At least this one was. There may be a crowd at the front door with expensive tickets in hand, but waiting at the office door was the lot owner with his hand out, the hay man, the supplier of the donikers, the high-priced stranger-gouging town mechanics, even a few corrupt politicians.

We lost money on the VIP passes, but we had to give them out for "favors." There were real hazards: equipment breaking down, motors, transmissions, brakes, power systems, not to speak of rigging.

Yesterday, Chris's gear became entangled. When the men tried to get the block and tackle free, they bent her rigging. That meant her act had to be cancelled until it could be straightened out or replaced.

Everyone was exhausted, but the greatest danger of all besides fire, wind and storm was wrecking the trucks. If Bryan dumped the van over and Neena was badly injured, she would have to be destroyed. That would wipe out the show.

Red and Bryan pushed themselves compulsively. They were apologetic about even pulling over for a few minutes. It seemed so important to race on to the next town, be the first one on the new lot, like a bunch of wild horses stampeding to an oasis in the middle of the desert.

There were smaller dangers, too.

"Where does Sparky sleep?" I asked Bob just before we pulled out.

"In the sleeper with the men."

"What if Sparky wandered off and met up with a skunk? You know there's a lot of them out here in the country."

Bob was silent, but we both knew it would be a disaster.

We ran a clean circus—no gambling, grift or grime. Maybe just a little too much dust.

There's a world of difference between circus and carnies. Yesterday, a carnie stopped by the door.

"I retired in 1972, but I'll do my act for you free, and if you like it—"

"You have to see Red." That was my tape recording answer. It made life on the door more tolerable. Everyone had to "see" Red.

You could see Red a mile off with that flaming shock of carrot hair, the red-white complexion, the light blue eyes that gave him a wild, frightened rabbit look.

You could see Red in the ring, a blaze of color in his orange spangled topcoat two sizes too big for him and that stovepipe of a hat.

You could see Red on the midway behind a microphone, spieling his sideshow. But catching him to talk to him took skill.

However, the carnie was a pro. He nailed Red between the sideshow and the ring. Red's face remained expressionless. I don't think he liked carnies. Red was a "circus" man, and a purist at that, like John. Carnival to them was a racket. Circus was an art.

Later, the carnie floated back to my ticket stand.

"What did Red say?" I asked.

"He said it was too bizarre for him."

"What do you do?"

"I stick pins in my face."

"Really?" I was unimpressed. Jim's blockhead act with the ice pick was pure fakery. All he did was slip it up his nose into the nasal cavity. Geeks went out with the Depression. I knew what a geek was. I'd seen the movie, *Nightmare Alley*. Tyrone Power was down and out and bit the heads off of live chickens for a living. Others swallowed frogs, even snakes. I sort of lumped pin stickers with geeks.

"Yeah," he said beaming a gold-toothed smile, "I don't fake it." There were fresh needle holes in one side of his cheek, complete with bits of dried blood.

23

The circus is supposed to be light-hearted and gay, but just as it is for us on the show—sometimes tragedy lies just beyond the canvas. So it is with towners along the way.

Being on the front door night after night, I had an excellent opportunity to observe people. Their faces often reflected their own personal tragedies.

Sometimes it was an old man with a large ugly skin cancer spreading across his face, eating him up day by day. He would come to the circus, trying to find a moment's freedom from the pain of dying, but even the circus couldn't drive away death.

Sometimes it was a young mother recently abandoned, trying hard to push away the reality of having to be father and mother both.

Then there were the children.

Battered children have blackened eyes and visible facial lacerations. These are the children who have been slapped broad-handed by a large adult. Often, rough little guys passed through the gate with shiners, but they strutted proudly. They'd earned their black eyes messing it up with some neighborhood bully.

Two beautiful blond children, brother and sister, about four years old, approached me timidly—sadly. Their parents were right behind them. I had to take a second look. It might not have been noticeable to see one child with a shiner, but both of these children had puffy eyes, swollen tissue turning blackish purple and cuts. Two children from the same family with identical wounds made it difficult to believe it was an accident.

I called the sponsor over. She agreed with me that it looked suspicious.

She spoke to the police officer who stood nearby to control the crowds. He sent me into the tent to check where they had taken seats. I patrolled the crowd until I located the family, way down at the far end. Satisfied that they were in the tent and there was something to what I'd told him, the cop walked in himself and saw the strange bruises. Then he requested someone from Juvenile to assist him.

At intermission, a female officer in plain clothes came from the Juvenile Division. She intercepted the family on the midway. I watched from the bus window as she asked the little girl a lot of questions, but the baby was either too frightened or too shy to say much. She stood there, head bowed, and shook her head very slowly.

The father stood with his arms folded. The mother did most of the talking. While the officers talked to the children, the father nervously stepped over to the concession wagon and returned with his hands full of cotton candy and drinks for the children. They couldn't say much with their mouths full of spun sugar. I don't think he had bought anything before that because their faces were clean except for the bruises.

After it was over, I caught up with the female officer and apologized if I had called her out needlessly.

"No, you did the right thing," she said, smiling. "We wish more people would call us."

"I think the children recover from the wounds but the parents don't. The guilt destroys them."

"Not all the kids recover," she said sadly. Then she patted me on the arm. "You did the right thing."

"What did the parents say?"

"Mosquito bites."

"What do you think?"

"The officers and I thought there was reason to investigate. We'll keep them under surveillance now."

The show was over. The tent was down. Red took personal charge of picking up every last cotton candy cone. There was at least a one hundred dollar cleaning deposit on every lot we played. John Strong prided himself that in over twenty-five years he'd never had to forfeit a cleaning deposit. After the reel truck scooped up the folded canvas, there would be no evidence left that a circus had ever come to town.

The men were tired and cross. Everyone snapped, even Jim when I reported the electric cord to the office had shorted out. I traced the extension cord, past about a dozen knots that no one took time to untie, to a big tangled bulge with bare wires exposed. The strain of the knot had literally severed the cord in two. Quickly, I unplugged it from the breaker box. I didn't know much about electricity, but just the night before, the large expensive quartz lamp on the midway had sputtered and sparked when some kids shook it. Curtis said there was enough amperage in it to kill someone. He had Jim check it out immediately.

When I told Jim that I condemned the cord and had unplugged it, he snapped back at me, "I haven't time to fix it!"

Accidents on the show were just one way a circus could die.

We played Winnemucca on a Saturday afternoon, unusually early, one and three P.M. shows. The tent was down by five. I tried to sleep while Curtis counted up, but I was still shaken over the bruised children. Sandy had come nosing around while the cops were talking to the children. I wondered if in any way she tied me into the whole thing. I doubt if she or Red would've approved of me sticking my nose in other people's business, especially when it involved the cops, or was on company time. Sandy was always put out with me, and with Curtis for something, mostly because Curtis had trouble getting a hold of sponsors in time for her to get directions straight.

We had set up in a parking lot of the Winnemucca speedway. Red and the rest pushed on toward Elko, where Red had given the single men on the show liberty to take in some Nevada style fun. By the time we had finished post-show Pie Car, the lot was filling up with stock car race fans. Curtis suggested we go watch the races, but I was too upset and tired, so he went alone.

When I woke up, he still wasn't back, so I went looking for him, just in time for the last race. The winner broke an axle on the last lap but hung on to the finish with a tie rod dragging and sparks flying.

I looked at Curtis. His shoulders were drooping and his face pale. I hadn't realized how tired he was getting, but the diversion had done him good. It was more refreshing than extra sleep.

We were really too tired to drive on to Elko, but if we didn't, we wouldn't make Pie Car on time in the morning. Once asleep, we just couldn't get up again.

I felt like rebelling, pulling onto the KOA down the street, plugging in, taking a shower, washing the clothes and sleeping through the Elko stand. Then, all we'd have to do was drive as far as Battle Mountain, which was halfway. The circus had to double back over itself tomorrow night in order to go north toward Oregon.

But we couldn't afford to miss any more stands under any circumstances. I guess if we broke down we might hitchhike with pies in hand.

When Curtis started up the bus I wondered if we would pass anyone on the way. I hoped not. They should all be in Elko by now if someone hadn't fallen asleep at the wheel.

Bryan would be terribly tired. Like an old mother hen, I had clucked a warning to Red.

"There should always be a co-driver on those heavy trucks. I never let Curtis drive alone."

"I don't want anyone with me!" Red snapped sharply. But as Bryan pulled out with the elephant van, I had seen Bob up in the cab beside him.

When we finally pulled into Elko, the arrows were all messed up. Sandy had put the first turn arrows on the sign "after" the turn-off! We sailed on by before we saw them. We took the next turn-off and doubled back until we found the arrows again. That small detail at three in the morning was giving me an ulcer.

We followed the arrows. Finally, we stopped at a gas station and asked.

They said we were the fifth vehicle that had stopped and asked. Let's see, I took mental count: One—Red and the reel truck, two—Bryan and the elephant van, three—Jim and the sleeper, four—Prince and the side show trailer, five—Ron and Chris, six—Tina in the bread truck with the bear, seven—Sandy in the sound car, and us. That made eight. Curtis Cainian and Sherry, the ninth vehicle, were still back in Winnemucca. I wondered if anyone had found the lot.

I don't know who was at fault—Sandy for failing to put the arrows up right or Curtis for not getting instructions from the sponsor.

I sat staring at the snow-covered Ruby Mountains off in the distance. Elko had become a boomtown. People spent money freely. Both shows filled to capacity. There were no advance sales, but everyone had read the newspaper and cut out the coupons.

Red was ecstatic. The candy butchers were kept moving. But I worked the door in tears.

Curtis had told me we were quitting the show.

"It's only a matter of time," he said. "My right lung is hurting all the time now. If I had an X-ray, I'm sure there'd be a spot on it."

We told Sandy that afternoon. She begged us to stay on if we could.

"There's no one else who can do you guys's job. Everyone else has to perform in the show."

We promised to think it over, and give her two weeks notice. Our conversation was cut short when Sandy and I heard our cue. Hand in hand, Sandy and I ran for the main tent. She had to get Bob's straitjacket and I had to recruit two volunteers from the audience.

I was struggling for breath, but I'd beat her out by a belly roll. More important—we didn't miss our cue.

I would miss the circus if we left. No matter how difficult things became, or how angry I was, I would miss the circus—my circus. I looked around me. The shabby, torn canvas sidewalls flapped loudly in the wind. I was all choked up, but it wasn't pollen.

Billy came by with his helicopter beanie spinning. He smiled up at me like an innocent cherub. I thought of Rudolph Del Monte, who we all called Pinky, when he was growing up on the Circus Vargas lot. Rudolph was a man now, with his own contortion act. Just yesterday, Pinky was a little boy like Billy, playing in the circus "backyard."

Neena tugged at her iron bracelet. The bear moaned from his cage and the ewe bleated complaints because the rams were in the arena without her.

I cleaned up the midway and scurried through the dust from the sanctuary of my bus. Just as I slid under the bed, looking for another six-pack of Coke, there was a knock at the door. The Riveras wanted four cups of coffee and four Sloppy Joes. Red was fast on their heels with his giant cup. I really should've charged him more, but the coffee was lousy. When I get some more good coffee I'll raise the price.

I'd already had to raise the price of the pies to seventy-five cents. Even then, I wasn't making my "nut money" on the Pie Car. Ever since Bryan went on the wagon and the sale of beer came to a squeaking halt, I'd been going downhill. They had gotten tired of bologna sandwiches, even ham and cheese. The only things that were still popular were fried chicken and Sloppy Joes.

In the spewing out of complaints to Sandy, the matter of the Pie Car's dwindling profits was mentioned, but far more important was the strained relations with Chris.

It began when Red came over to Pie Car and asked if we'd make a sign.

"Make it—HELP WANTED," he said, "and put a little humor in it."

I did. The sign read:

HELP WANTED. NO BRAINS, JUST BRAWN.

When Chris saw the sign posted on the front of the office van, she scratched out the last part.

"She took it as an insult," Curtis said. "No one works any harder than Chris around here."

"I did exactly what Red had said. I understood he wanted towner day labor. That's what he got, too. I see they put a temporary man on this morning.

Good worker. He didn't seem pushed out of shape by the sign. It simply meant we needed hard-working, strong laborers."

"Somewhere she got the idea we think we could run this show better than she can."

"That has nothing to do with it. We weren't advertising for office personnel, just canvasmen and stakedrivers. She doesn't do that kind of work."

Nevertheless, the die was cast. The hand had to be played out. Nobody could win the pot. The circus would lose us and we would lose the circus.

I thought of the auto race we had stopped to watch last night. The winning car took the last laps with a broken tie rod and the wheel laid over at an angle, but he got the checkered flag for hanging in there.

The Bible said to run the race till the finish. There were other cars in the race. They spun out in order to race another day.

I peeped through the window. The men were lined up each at his station.

They pulled on the canvas in unison, calling their ancient chant. They laughed and smiled as they worked, even though we were all bone-tired.

They were a brave bunch. Each one must have his own reason for continuing this adventure.

I didn't want to quit yet. But if things didn't improve by Albany, Oregon, that was the cut-off point for us. The circus would go north and we'd go back to California.

We got to Battle Mountain last because we stopped to eat in a restaurant. All the same, we got a full night's sleep even if it did little good by now. I couldn't control the shaking inside, dizziness, lack of coordination, weakness—feeling of fainting. It was like one big hangover, but all it could be described as was collective fatigue, like battle fatigue. It was a physical tiredness, but an emotional one, too. The entire morale was low. Half the show had colds.

However, Bryan felt better. I asked him how come.

"Got my beer back," he said, strutting off.

Bryan strutted, so did Peewee. Red walked head down, shoulders forward like a sailor leaning into the wind. Tom minced. Chris walked on her heels, chest out, head up. Sandy picked her way along, always on high heels, like a beautiful queen. Carmen just slopped along.

It was 9:30 P.M. when the people returned from intermission. That was because the show didn't start until 8:30! That made it hard on everyone. I could only hope one of the acts was cut short and we could still get out on time. Tina went on for her swinging trapeze just as I left for the bus.

The Riveras came for coffee and fried chicken.

"Do you have one sack with all drumsticks?" Ernie asked. He was always the one out of step. If I had plenty of pies but no chocolate, he wanted chocolate.

His brother wanted only lemon.

"No!" I shouted angrily. "One drumstick, one wing, one breast and one back. That's how God made the chicken and that's what's fair!" Then as an aftermath I added, "But there's no necks." I halfway expected him to say he liked necks.

"Better take something for morning," I said.

"Why?"

"No Pie Car."

Curtis had decided we would make a pit stop in Winnemucca. It was that or quit the show right now. We were too dogtired, dirty, out of clothes and out of sorts.

Sparky was dogtired too. He laid down on the sideshow bally platform and went into a coma.

I saw a little girl jump when she discovered him. "Is that dog dead?" she cried out in alarm.

"Just dead tired," I said. "He had a hard night." I guess he was just as tired as everyone else on the show.

Only three months out of winter quarters and there wasn't any of us, including Neena, who didn't feel like quitting, especially Jim.

Jim had always seemed the calmest one, seldom complaining, always busy. He was a good juggler, great clown, a terrific side show speaker, a fair electrician and the safest driver we had on the show. He was up at six thirty each morning to lay out stakes, swinging a twenty pound hammer until the anchor stakes were all in place. He heaved and ho-ed with the rest, but when they napped in the afternoon, he was usually busy repairing the lights or that infernal wiring. He alternated with Red on the sideshow, did the blockhead act with the ice pick up his nose, and then did a production number in center ring with BJ besides his regular rola bola juggling act.

But tonight for some reason, Jim Zajicek, was absent from the sideshow. I looked for him out back, then I got busy taking tickets on the door. I saw him streaking out from the sleeper. No one was taking quarters for the sideshow! We were losing enough money on the show without giving a free sideshow on the midway. I yelled at him. There was a moment of confusion. Several people guiltily exited from the trailer. One of the Riveras came around the corner just in time to see what was going on. He positioned himself by the door and the people filed in, dropping coins in his hand. Red came out of the tent with a storm cloud on his face. I could see him chewing Ernie out. There was no time to ask questions. Ernie, I had just found out, was the name of the Rivera with the long beard whom I had began calling Prince after he was no longer Muhammed. Ernie wasn't as romantic a name as Prince.

Everything seemed to be going wrong. Everyone was bone tired and didn't know what to do about it.

Little irritating things happened. One of the goats kept slipping his leash. He had learned to crawl under the concession trailer where we couldn't reach him.

BJ, who usually was so even-going and expressionless, stampeded around like an outraged bull. He couldn't find his props. They'd been transported in the small truck. But the small truck was still in the shop back in Winnemucca. He missed his cue. Then he dismantled the sleeper looking for something, probably more props. Sandy howled, "Get your ass in gear, BJ, and go in there and finish your act!"

24

There is, no matter how fine a show put on, something missing for someone.

"Where are the toilets?"

"Didn't you see them as you came in?"

"No," the lady said, trying to hold on to a twisting, turning tot grabbing the crotch of his pants.

"There's donikers usually out front."

"I…he has to go bad."

"Ma'am, the donikers are out front." I really hoped the portable toilets had been delivered. I was the one who got the short end of the stick over them. Nobody ever complained to the manager about the lack of proper toilet facilities. They always nailed me because I was on the door—convenient, and I suppose wearing a pitiful look that vaguely resembled compassion.

"He can't wait!" she said as she dragged him behind a flap of midway canvas.

When we played schools, the janitors often left the lavatories open. When we played fairgrounds, there were, almost without any exceptions, adequate facilities because they serviced steady flows of fair crowds. But rodeo grounds, sand lots and open fields near shopping centers required us renting portable toilets which circus people called donikers.

Some towns were so small the donikers had to be ordered from another town nearby or the nearest city. Sometimes they didn't arrive the day we did. They never could understand that we played just one day or one night stands. One thing could be counted on—they all charged by the week and a minimum of two units. It was fruitless to try explaining to them that we could only use the donikers for one night.

Another thing missing was a well-stocked menagerie. Every circus had to have animals. In fact, our contract called for an elephant on duty at all times, plus horses. I don't think anything was mentioned about Bonzo the bear or the goats. The less said about them the better. I knew Tina didn't have time to train them properly, but in three months, all the little bear could do was stand up on its hind legs and drink from a baby bottle. As far as the goats were concerned, they were darling. I loved them, but their act consisted of Tina pulling them over a hurdle by a short tight leash. When she was angry, she could make those pygmy goats fly through the air like Peter Pan.

"Do you have animals?"

"Yes, we have animals."

"What?"

"An elephant, a bear, goats, ponies and horses," I said. Altogether, it sounded like we had something.

"No cats?"

"The animal trainer has two ferocious pussy cats. One of the cats has one blue eye and one…"

She walked away in disgust.

Not everyone wanting something is hostile. Sometimes there was a different routine on the door. A little girl breathlessly handed me two adult tickets. "It's for Cindy White," she said mysteriously. "You'll know her when you see her. She'll be along later." The girl vanished into the crowd. I held an extra ticket a few moments then dropped it into the bag. After all, she said I would "know" Cindy White.

I went about my business, collecting my tickets. Then the girl returned. "It's okay now. Cindy White is on the midway."

I fully expected nothing short of the Queen of England. Instead, I got a diminutive teenager in sweater and blue jeans with a bright smile on her face.

"I'm Cindy White!"

Of course she was Cindy White. I would know.

Neena broke into Peewee's van. Curtis said something about seeing Neena step on Garfield, but Billy filled in the details.

"I come for soup," he said.

"Isn't it a little late for you?"

"Nope." Billy held out a crumpled dollar. "And I want it in Mickey Mouse."

"You can't have Curtis's tippy cup any more. He wants it for when he's driving." I was referring to the kind of a trainer cup used for infants that had a secure lid on it and a small sipping hole. It worked fine while bouncing down the road.

Billy turned his lip down.

"Okay, you can have your soup in the Mickey Mouse tippy cup, but only if you wash it and bring it right back."

I put water on for his noodle soup.

"You know what Neena did?" Billy asked.

"I heard something."

"She broke into our van and stole my pennies."

"That all?"

"Nope. She got Scooby Doo and Garfield."

"Who's Scooby Doo?" I asked. I knew who Garfield was—that silly looking stuffed cat.

"Scooby Doo's a dog," Billy said, disgusted with my apparent ignorance. "Neena tore his tail off and Garfield's leg."

"Was she playing with your toys?"

He turned his hands up in the I-don't-know of a four year old.

Curtis's version was that he came around the corner and saw Neena playing with Billy's toys. I don't think she really meant to harm the dolls.

Little by little, I was being incorporated into the show. It was my job to listen and rush in breathless after Bob began his magic act. I would look slightly panicky and badger some unsuspecting patron into strapping Seaton into his strait jacket.

Another job was babysitting the goats. Twice today I had to chase down one of the pygmy goats. The last time, he ran into the crowd and one of the patrons helped me catch him. But this time I couldn't leave the gate, so I held the goat by his leash until Sandy came by to retrieve her goat.

"He attracted a nice crowd of kids to admire and pet him. Why don't I keep him here on a leash during intermission?"

"Fine," Sandy said, taking the goat's leash. "But this one nips. Better use Cricket. She's the one with the little brown mark on her backside."

Now I had a one-goat act all my own.

That night we doubled back to Winnemucca and checked into a KOA camp. Curtis was coughing now. He collapsed to sleep while I was enjoying the unusual luxury of a shower.

Curtis slept around the clock. Then after buying a much-needed new circuit breaker which couldn't be obtained in any small town, we left Winnemucca and our brief retreat and quickly covered the distance to the Oregon border in time to work the show in McDermitt.

Curtis rushed to Chris's trailer to get the money boxes, but they weren't there. Chris already had the office set up and was preparing to sell tickets.

"We thought you'd blown the show," she said, the extra tired showing on her face. "You should really stay with the show, you know. I shouldn't have to set up this office."

"You should have known I'd make it on time."

"But we found the posting you returned, and you collected for your gas last night."

"The posting's done, and we always collect on Mondays. Look, Chris, we'll give you plenty of notice. We're trying to hang in there. But we're about to the breaking point."

"Just about the whole show is," Chris said. She wasn't very sympathetic. Not everybody on the show understood.

The road to Burns was hell. We made it, but the winter rains and general neglect due to the cutback of government spending had turned Oregon State Highway 95 into a nightmare. Twice the dog bounced completely off the bed as we hit chuckhole after pothole. Some places, the road just wasn't even there any more. Others, the side of the mountain had slipped down and the road shoulders were strewn with boulders.

For it's a long way from Burns to Redmond with no gas stations in between—so goes the song.

At least it was for Sandy and Tina. We had found them parked beside a gas station, but a station that itself was out of gas. After siphoning off enough of our gas to get them to the next station, we followed them to where Carlos and the sideshow trailer were—also out of gas. There, all three waited together for the station to open. We went on. We carried eighty gallons. We never ran out of gas.

As we entered Bend, we came upon one of the big rigs of ours broken down. Bryan was so hoarse he could hardly talk.

"It's the drive shaft gone," he croaked faintly. "Hurry! Tell Red!"

Even though it was already eight-thirty in the morning, it would be well after ten before Jay would have started up the reel truck and moved it to tent location. Sandy, Tina and Carlos had finally arrived. It would take an earthquake to revive them. Their morale had dropped them so low, they weren't even speaking to each other, much less us, even though there had been a brief let-up in the cold war ever since we surprised them by showing up in McDermitt.

"We thought you left the show," Red said. The blue eyes were bluer than ever, but now bloodshot with fatigue. He was serious. He really was surprised to see us every time we showed up.

"No way. I'll let you know when I'm ready to give up," I said. "Besides, you guys all owe me too much money for Pie Car."

Poor Red. He crawled out of his warm sleeping bag to a freezing cold day, dark storm clouds and an elephant stranded up the road with a broken drive shaft.

He looked so little-boyish, the beautiful gold-red hair standing askew, those light blue eyes drowsy with sleep. He took the news calmly. He'd expected this long overdue breakdown. Either that, or he was in shock.

He sometimes got overexcited at the door around showtime. (Was it a good crowd? Would it be a full house?) But never when disaster surrounded us. Then he was our stormwise captain, calmly heading the ship into the wind and trimming her sails.

But our canvas didn't trim well. It lay on the ground in a shopping mall all day, with only the side poles in place. The next step was for Neena to pull the center poles up, but Neena was back in that broken down van.

I found a store to shop in and took Curtis with me to approve of a blue and white striped sailor shirt for nineteen dollars. That was a lot of money for a T-shirt. When we came out of the store, I yelled, pointing to the sky. "It's going to rain and the canvas is still on the ground!"

People—children—were walking all over the canvas. New holes appeared in the fast-rotting fabric. We'd do good to keep it over our heads the rest of the season.

"It's three P.M.!" I said, as we walked quickly back to the bus. "The tent's still down and I don't see anyone around."

"They're probably all asleep—all except Red. He's most likely back in Bend, trying to get that van down here," Curtis said.

It was way after three when a large tow truck pulled the still disabled elephant van onto the parking lot. Neena, the three ponies, four goats and five dogs were none the worse for wear, except for being shitty.

"Didn't Neena get restless?" I asked Red.

"No, not a bit. She was glad to be in out of the cold."

The biting wind snapped at the canvas as Neena pulled the center pole in place. We couldn't get the tent up without her. In fact, the show couldn't go on without the one elephant. It was in the contract. One thing for sure, we couldn't have called a cab for her. It had to be an expensive tow truck.

"Why didn't you get Ron to ride her up here?" I asked foolishly. "It would've made a good publicity stunt."

"She couldn't have made it all the way. She's not used to walking much."

"I'm not either, but I can move on out in a pinch."

I thought about the impromptu parade we could've caused. Like a Pied Piper, Neena could've led a huge crowd down to the circus lot. I watched Neena working. She was quite plump for a circus elephant. Maybe a few miles roadwork would be good for her.

Neena hoisted the center poles. The flags flew high. So did the wind. Before the block and tackle could be tightened, the wind flapped the canvas like a ship coming out of the doldrums.

"It's going!" I screamed. I was sure we would have our first blowdown. Nothing could be worse than having the canvas half up, half down.

A young man approached the bus.

"Can't you help?" I yelled out the window.

"I'm applying for work," he said. "I came for teardown."

"We need all the help we can get!" I shouted, feeling horror as I watched the tent threaten to collapse. "Get to work! Do something!"

The men tugged furiously. Some scurried like mice to unload the props from the disabled van. Instead of maneuvering around where they were needed, the props now had to be unloaded and toted by hand. They raced until minutes before show time, but we were rewarded as the crowd filed in.

The pre-sale of tickets had been excellent. There was a good crowd for the first show despite the bitter, freezing wind and sudden drops of rain.

"Where's a warm place to sit?" someone asked.

"See if you can find two fat ladies," I said straightfaced. "Squeeze in between them."

25

When we got to Newport, we declared ourselves a little holiday. We drove around and found the waterfront. While dining on seafood in Newport, watching sailboats frolicking in wisps of fog and whitecapped spume, I said to myself—what's a nice little girl like me doing following an elephant down the road every night?

Now that Neena's van had been fixed, Ron rolled down the road at the lead. So we were back to elephant following. But we let Neena go on ahead without us. We sacked in at a closed up bowling alley parking lot. The drive down Highway 20 was worth getting up early for. The lane-like country road wound around gentle green hills sloping down to the sea. We crossed small streams with mossy riverbanks and watched cows clinging to steep wooded cliffs.

After we played a Sunday matinee, we ended the day going back over the same road to get to Corvallis. We were on that same winding, heavily-trafficked road about ten miles out from Newport when we found Carlos and Bob standing beside the stranded side show trailer and pickup.

Curtis stopped, even though there was hardly enough shoulder for one vehicle, much less our huge fat bus. We tried to jump start it but the old pickup failed to respond.

Some time later, Ron Pace also stopped. The four men struggled to get the vehicle started while heavy holiday traffic roared by from both directions. All it would take was one lousy drunk coming around the corner to ram into the bus—our bus loaded to the gills with gasoline, and our men all working in front around the engine of the pickup.

Some cars slowed down, others sped up defiantly—hostile at us for blocking the road.

My own uncle Roy had died on a road like this. Thinking about it, knowing we were all dangerously tired, knowing also that we were completely blocking one lane of fast traffic—pushed my nerves to a breaking point.

The next day in Albany was a short one. We had electricity but I was too tired to type, as usual. I did get a lot of mending done on the sewing machine I'd dragged along. I guess that made me wardrobe mistress of sorts. I put a lot of patches on one of the men's pants and sewed on a few buttons.

We had a good crowd, almost a record take so far. That cheered everyone up, except for Sandy. She was in another foul mood because she'd been caught sleeping past showtime. Everyone had to be in makeup by half-past. When it was time for her to go on, she was found napping.

I envied her. I had a busy door and no sponsor. I had to rush to make my cue. Seaton was already half through the magic box act. He had already cut Tina into three sections before I entered the tent. I didn't waste any time. I grabbed two males standing nearest the front door and shoved them quickly under the net toward Sandy, who was holding Seaton's straitjacket.

After the show, Seaton, who was always so very friendly toward me, came over fuming mad.

"Don't you ever bring any crumbs like that!" he said. "I had everything so neat—the rigging—my costume. Then those…"

I hadn't even looked at them. I apologized. But for the second show, I had trouble getting any kind of assistance.

"Will you help us?" I pleaded. The man held a pretty little girl on his lap.

"I need a strong man to tie the magician in his strait jacket."

"I'm not very good at tying knots any more," he said, holding up one hand. All of the fingers were missing. This was logging country. Saw blade accidents were common.

I was still shaken when, back on the door, a large, rather bulbous man came out to smoke a cigarette.

"I hate circuses," he said. "I've always hated them, but my son insisted we go."

He got my full attention. "Why do you hate circuses?"

"I don't know. I've always hated them. My parents forced me to go."

"Maybe that's why."

"No," he said scowling. "I hate to shop or go into any kind of crowded place."

I thought—he's a true agoraphobic. I could understand and sympathize. I felt the same way at times.

"I know," I said. "Sometimes I have trouble with grocery shopping. That's why I like to go in the wee hours of the morning whenever I can find an all night store."

But it was little consolation. He walked away, not back into the tent, but out across the field. Later on, from the bus window, I could see him wandering around. He'd paid four fifty to not see a circus.

We were now into territory where Spitt and Dixie had done the Advance.

"I don't believe it!" Red said hoarsely with that sweet, soft voice hoarse from smoking and spieling, always tinged with excitement, anticipation, hurry-hurry-step-right-up-folks-welcome-to-the-greatest-little-tent-show-in-the-world in his voice.

It was true. We had a record crowd both shows. By the time I made Pie Car and fried up chicken, I was so tired I had the screaming meemies. My hair was dirty, I was dirty, my husband was dirty and so was my dog. But we were all a little happier about the record crowd.

It was early afternoon before we got away from the lot. Curtis had just put new spark plugs on the sideshow camper. Little did he know he'd just promoted himself from office manager to circus wagon mechanic. Now that they knew he knew the difference between an Allen wrench and a screwdriver, he'd be asked to miraculously put all this rolling junkyard back together again.

If we could only beat the physical fatigue, we could make the whole season. We had come to love the routine, always the same, yet every day different. One of the routines was that each night the sponsor was ceremoniously given a ride on Neena, the elephant. Tonight, when it came time to ride her, the sponsor was conveniently absent. Later, Curtis asked him why.

"My ex-wife and my girlfriend are both in there watching the show," he explained. "I'm living with my ex-wife again and I don't want my girlfriend to find out."

And then there were some routines I could've done without. Sometimes I got sick and tired of listening to the sideshow lies. I wondered each day what it was that held the incoming crowd spellbound.

Just like children are calmed by fairy tales, adults get a much needed sense of community and continuity from being lied to, whether the circus midway or religion. That's the form of illusion.

But there's a therapeutic value in enchantment. Just as a parent and child can share and examine—albeit obliquely—the entire range of human problems, including a peek at the dark side, the unknown faces of humanity, which people need to do in order to come to terms with who they are. So with the circus—the fairy tale of the sideshow has its appeal.

"See Johnny Eck, the half-man"—"Jolly Joyce, five hundred and sixty pounds of feminine beauty"—"Jojo, the dog-faced boy"—"the bearded lady"—"the man with three legs."

They walk away whole, satisfied that they aren't freaks themselves.

During the second show I got some time to do some of the mending for the men. Jay's pants were done and he asked for a price.

"What's it worth to you?"

He hum-hawed around and said he'd be by the next day. I didn't want to charge for an act of love. But how could any of them know it was an act of love, including coffee at six A.M., when I loved to sleep in.

Bob drifted by with Sandy not far behind. For a change, they weren't fighting.

"Hey, Cookie," Sandy said, smiling. "How's about me doing Pie Car and you shoveling elephant—you know—stuff?"

"Me...shovel shit?" I pretended to be mortified.

"See, Seaton, what we've done to her. When she first came on the show, she called it excrement. Now she says 'shit.'"

I've kept saying the circus was a disaster waiting to happen. We were coming down the freeway when all of a sudden, I see the elephant van on the edge of the road. Elephant van—motor running—no air—headaches and dizziness—sleepy!

Bryan and BJ were both sound asleep or unconscious. The motor was running. Bryan was afraid to shut it off for fear it wouldn't start again. We checked Neena. She didn't seem to be groggy. But with a head as big as hers how could one tell if an elephant was groggy?

We stood by until Bryan woke up and we knew he was all right.

The name of the next town promised such a beautiful vision—Goldendale. Before the day was over, we would never forget Goldendale.

We climbed until the snow-capped mountains were no longer towering above us, but were beside us and we were a mingled part of them.

The cold wind, wild and fierce, began before dawn—first a breeze, then a gale—blustering, capricious, vicious. I fed the men their breakfast after stakes were driven and the canvas laid out on the ground. They were running late. The wind had rocked and buffeted the bus like an infant's cradle, lulling me back into a half-sleep even with Shadow barking furiously.

There seemed a note of hesitancy—then warning—to his rapid barking, but then Sparky was outside running around loose. Then I heard a furious slapping like a drummer on traps. The American flags were drumming against the canvas, a cadence of impending disaster. The wind was too high to finish getting the tent up!

Men stood still in awesome silence as the wind created a huge vacuum, sucking the air upward, billowing the canvas. Peewee's portable radio blared ugly rock music. The nasty, violent sound stood alone against the wind.

I grabbed my jacket and a windbreaker cap. Despite the penetrating cold, I wanted a ringside seat to what would happen next.

The men seemed hypnotized by the danger. The far section of canvas already hoisted on the quarterpoles dropped to the ground.

Surprisingly, Neena remained calm. It took more than a gale wind to budge two tons of elephant. Slowly, she began working without command. She tugged at the center pole, bringing it up into place. Ron's attention had been diverted by the canvas falling over what could be the "blues." But Neena knew what had to be done. She had tugged that pole in place thousands of times. She got that center pole in place so the men could stretch the canvas.

It was soft, slack canvas that was so treacherous. It pocketed the wind, turned it into a powerful dynamo that, if with but only a slight breeze, could drive a mighty ship across an ocean.

Neena's motion revived the men's spirits. In awesome silence they held onto the heavy poles until, one by one, Neena tugged them all into place. Now came the tugging and shouting. Groups of three men manned their battle stations at each dangling rope. They tugged and chanted until the slack was taken up, no longer afraid.

But the wind sang a song of promise—survival only of the fittest. The canvas was new and strong in the center. But at the far ends, the pieces were old and rotting. The wind promised to destroy and conquer if she got her chance.

The flags stood sentry, rat-tat-tatting a constant message of alarm. Only Red, more wild-eyed than ever, taking just one moment for a fresh cup of coffee, listened.

"Wait until we get to Wyoming," he said. "We'll have emergency teardowns. This'll happen in the middle of a show. We have to get the people out and collapse the tent without anybody getting hurt." Then I knew. I had to stay with the show. I wouldn't miss all of this for anything in the world.

We couldn't find Sunnyside. We weren't lost. The town was. On the map, it seemed so easy to get to, but when we came to a junction, we went left instead of right, then in a complete circle until we ended up right back where we started from. In the process, we met the sleeper bus coming toward us—also lost. I think between the two vehicles, we made a perfect figure eight.

There's no telling what misadventure Red and the reel truck had when they came to that junction. All I know was they were the last wheels in.

I was mad at the whole bunch. I got stuck for five orders of Sloppy Joes. I hoped the whole darn show chased their tails until dawn. But the next day, Red didn't even come for coffee and Bob was sick, so I dropped the whole matter. I just wouldn't cook chicken tomorrow. They could eat leftover Sloppy Joes all week.

It's strange, the chain of thoughts that enter the mind. I was glad to crawl up into the new arm chair by the window. Curtis had stopped and bought it because I needed it so badly. I watched the crowd leave, Red man his station on the side show and the men begin to load props.

Tina strutted by in a wild-colored sarong.

"See—Jolly Joyce, five hundred and sixty pounds of feminine beauty. On the inside, folks," Red sang in his bally.

Was he saying her beauty was on the inside?

I was Jolly Joyce on the outside but the incredible impossible dream of a Tina on my inside.

People entered and left the side-show. Bob practiced handstands as the last of the stragglers held on to a few more precious moments of the magic of the circus. This was Sunday night. The alternatives were: go home to an empty house, go to a bar and stare at a wet glass all evening or go to church. The circus was friendlier, cheaper and more tranquillizing.

Red popped in and out of the sideshow trailer. Business was good today, weather was warm and no wind.

My thoughts roamed wild like prairie stallions. I was terribly tired. With the constant numbness and tingling in my hands and feet, and the resultant panic and depression, I felt every one of my fat fifty-one years. I had worked too hard, been too many places at once, worried too much about possibly being crippled up from the constant whiplash injuries I had suffered on the trip.

Sponsors were sometimes worse than not having sponsors. Every time I took my eye off my helper, I saw someone slip through the unguarded gate. There seemed to be no correlation in their minds between taking tickets and making a buck.

"See the side show freaks," I heard Red say.

I was a freak, out of step with the whole cockeyed world. I was too fat, too old, too tired.

Jim came to the door for a soda. "Tired, huh?"

"Terribly. That was a workout—such a big crowd. I feel my age," I said, sitting back down in my new cozy high-backed lounge chair. All it needed was a rosy fire on the hearth, a cup of good tea and a fat white cat sitting in the window sunning herself.

"I have children older than anyone on this show. Linda is thirty-three."

"Red's only thirty-two. Gosh, I didn't know that. You don't look your age."

"I have a grandson eleven and a granddaughter three." I meant it more as a complaint against the years than a grandmotherly brag.

"I'm waiting to just be an uncle," Jim said. "You know—the kind that shows up at family get-togethers—reunions—and tells the children a bunch of tall stories."

I could see Jim with a big cigar in his mouth and a little tot on each knee, telling them how once he was a juggler in the circus.

And to my own grandchildren in the future, not Linda's or Donna's children, but maybe David's, Don's or Danny's, I will say:

This fat little grandmother ran away and joined a circus, kiddies. No, not as a Fat Lady, you little twirp. I was a few pounds short.

"What did you do in the circus, grandma?" someone would say.

Just about everything. And so—an impossible dream. Little old ladies don't run away from home and join a circus, or do they?

26

It was only a few more miles on a Sunday evening under a lovely full moon—misty moon like in a Japanese painting—lacy moon covering her face with a fan of clouds. We slept instead of having our usual moon date. It had been a sweet ritual ever since we had gotten married. Now, sleep was more precious than romance.

I woke up feeling much better. Two new men had been put on the crew. The first—Dave, I didn't like. He was big, violent, threatening and drank continually. I caught him tippling in the sleeper from one of those Portuguese flasks—a bladder-shaped thing. I don't have anything against drinking, but not on the job, not in front of the children.

The second man had been put on late last night. I hadn't learned his name, but I liked him. He looked like he was used to hard work and he didn't grumble. The other one—the one who drank, grumbled.

It was a lovely bright morning. The sky was clear blue, the grass, green, no harsh noises except Peewee's loud portable radio, but no rock music this morning. Thank God for small favors.

Neena trumpeted, the dogs barked and the van's motor growled like a wounded lion. Neena trumpeted again in sympathy, but the diesel had died. It was a miracle it had gotten this far without breaking down.

Somehow, we'd all made it this far.

The next day began the business of No Pie Car. It's hard to define where or why. The unclaimed Sloppy Joes that had been ordered but never picked up or paid for, the clodhopper towner Ernie, who came for teardown but hung around the gate, jabbering and driving me nuts. Ernie always was "sure" I didn't have lemon pies or hot coffee.

Then the midway lights came crashing down, scattering shattered slivers of glass everywhere. It fell right where I usually stood to take tickets. Only, because I couldn't get rid of Ernie, and he continued his vigil on the midway, even when I took my break—the lights fell on him.

I stormed back to the bus. Peewee saw me go. He heard me too because I was cussing the whole damned circus. Then came the tears. I howled. The dog howled. We bayed together like hounds under a full moon.

Curtis gave Red a two-week notice. He had continued to weaken. We would leave the show in Idaho before we got any farther away from California. Without the responsibility of doing Pie Car, we found more and more excuses to spend every moment we could away from the circus lot.

We slept in Walla Walla and spent the day under a huge shade tree. The neighborhood we chose was like a typical Midwestern rural town with old houses, older trees, middle-aged rose bushes and ancient ivy. It took time to grow rosebushes and decades for a wall to become covered with ivy.

There was a great beauty in permanence, like river rocks that don't shatter. Depression and wars come, famine and natural disasters, too, but those rocky old walls remained.

We were able to see the rolling countryside by daylight. Green hills, green waves of high grass contouring the land like marcelles on a head of hair. Winding brooks along the roadway, telling the road where to go, leading the way to another town. Towns strung along the road like tiny pearls on an old-fashioned necklace.

When we came to the junction of Highway 26, the sleeper bus and Red's reel truck had pulled over because Marian and Carlos were out of gas. The junction station was closed until morning.

"Can we siphon?" Marian asked.

Curtis started the hose for her. I gave him Pepsi to rinse the gasoline out of his mouth. We didn't mind giving them gas, but they sure hated waiting for it to siphon out.

"If we were going to stay with this show, I'd get a real siphon and turn us into a rolling filling station."

But we were definitely leaving. I had told Dixie earlier that evening. She understood.

"We aren't circus. I did my best, but it wasn't good enough."

Several things of significance happened in Othello: the taking down of Pie Car signs, the beer empties on the midway and—Curtis relieved of morning call-in.

Last night, when Marian ran out of gas, she and Carlos patiently siphoned seventeen gallons from our tank, but in departing, insisted on paying us for our "time." The gas belonged to the circus.

Perhaps she didn't realize how permanently she was cutting us off. We were towners once again. We had never really been "circus." That, too, like everything else, was just an illusion.

The sights and sounds of circus that I loved so much now became torturous sounds, irritating and discordant. I tried to drown out the sound of Red's beautiful voice.

The hours on the door became tense. I scowled at Red.

"See Blockhead," Red said hoarsely. "The man who makes Pinocchio look intelligent."

It was getting to them, too. I broke out laughing.

We slept that night at Moses Lake in a field of volcanic ash. We woke up to a bright quiet Sunday morning—a good time for introspection.

Every time I called the show a bunch of ring ponies, Curtis thought I said it with a hint of sarcasm. But I wasn't being cruel or sarcastic. There was good to be said of the herd instinct, communal feeling—togetherness.

Tina came by, breathless and sweaty. She'd been chasing her ponies all over the place.

"Now that John is coming down," she complained, "we have to put the figure eight back in the act. The ponies don't like it. They keep jumping the ring curb and running away."

That's what we were planning to do—jump the curb and run away.

That night, when we sat down to eat, I opened my Bible to the twelfth chapter of Hebrews. "What's a race?" I asked Curtis.

He read the chapter again. As usual, he was slow to answer—meditative. Then he said, looking away, "Making it to the end of the season."

We had wondered what Soap Lake was like. That's what the water felt like—being in soap suds. It wasn't a very pretty lake—no moss-covered banks or luxuriant tree growth, just a few trees on the far side like a fringe of hair over the ears of a bald man. But at night, the lights across the lake fell in pretty multicolored patterns upon the water.

I rose early in the morning. It was barely five A.M. We had pulled into the camper parking area next to the city park where the circus was to be set up.

We were far enough away to not be disturbed, but close enough for it to still be disturbing. Already, I could make out the figures of Red and Bryan laying out the dye markers on the ground for the tent poles.

Sparky frisked after the men with his huge orange plume of a tail bouncing high. I could hear the throb-throb-throb heartbeat of the big truck even from such a distance. But then, I thought I would hear it forever, just like a deaf mother with full breasts hears her baby cry.

I felt unbearable sadness. Ron would go get doughnuts. Chris would dutifully pour coffee from a thermos. They were young and strong and would survive. They didn't need me like I needed them. No one cared.

I would return to my books—musty books and mustier libraries and the voice of the reel truck would diminish. It had been a grand crazy adventure, but it was survival of the fittest, and we weren't very fit at all.

I sat in the bus, curtains drawn, with only a small window bared to the blue lake. It was stifling, airless, except in the slipstream of the small fan aimed mercifully toward Curtis. He sat in silence reading, not protesting. We were shut off from the whole world.

I could hear Neena trumpeting all the way across the lake. I dressed quickly and stepped out to the lake's edge to see what was going on.

Neena stood belly deep in the cool lake, tossing water over her back with her trunk. Nearby, Peewee and Ron were playing with a huge beach ball. Neena playfully squirted them with a strong jet of water. They romped and frolicked, others joining them until the whole show was in the water. Ron gave Neena her cue and she began dancing in the shallow water.

Tears formed in my eyes. It was a beautiful scene I would always remember. They were all so young and strong and full of hope. The circus was no place for an emotional old woman. They didn't need me. They didn't want a mother any more than my own grown children did.

The wind drove the placid waters in our direction, like a river making herringbone patterns across its shimmering surface. The light fog had lifted, revealing blue skies. These, in turn, were reflected upon the water. It turned to soft hazy blue. Now the lake held a soft mild beauty as if a homely woman had fallen in love.

The lake flowed in the direction of the sea, not the feminine sea, but the masculine El Mar, as if to form a marriage alliance—a strange misogynistic relationship of soda springs and sea. Then I thought of the words to a song, "Cry Me a River." I'll cry a deep blue sea.

Curtis had found me singing Irish lullabies last night when he returned to the bus. My mind had slipped back to times past—to when the children were babies.

Then the scene changed and fantasy took over. I was in another century. The cabin's roof was thatched and covered with clods of sod. On one side, the roof sloped nearly to the ground and seemed to join the hillside.

Ellen Durstyn (that's who I felt like being) sat beside the hearth, her mending in her lap. She gazed at the coals and daydreamed of John Gunny from Keogh.

He was her father's foreman, a rugged man with huge powerful shoulders and a trim waist, but legs as stout as oaks and sinew like a mountain goat. His father before him had been a herdsman and a foreman. They had no inheritance of their own, only their fierce Scottish pride. They worked for the large landowners but they were no lief men. The stout men from Keogh were free and bold and had a fierce love for the land they cared for.

Ellen saw flames leap from one rekindled coal. John of Keogh's hair was a fiery coal burning brightly. His eyes were an incredible light blue, his cheeks as pink as a blushing schoolboy. He *was* Red Johnson!

The long barren drive up to Grand Coulee was frightening. The land was so wild and desolate. The bus was running ragged and had very little power. It was hot and humid. It seemed that our time left with the show was all downhill from here on in. It was no time to have a breakdown. We seemed to be having ignition problems.

Two more towns flew by. Two more nights of the same performance, the same words, the same type crowds. Word came down the line that John would appear on the show in Kellogg, Idaho. We were being replaced a week earlier than we thought.

We were a mess. There was a coating of fine dust on everything—the wall, the books, the carpet. There were streaks of ugly black grease on my best negligee. The dog would run under the bus, then come in and rub the grease on whatever I was wearing. Grease, dirt, mud, sand, volcanic ash—the bus was saturated with parts of Arizona, California, Nevada, Oregon, Washington and Idaho.

The last two weeks I have been having some time to get the ring curb dust out of my eyes. I concocted a story to tell at the door that we were soon retiring. I began planning a new book to write.

Maybe the day would come when circus music, the blare of Red's voice on the midway, Bob's stentorian call for the elephant rides and the constant deafening roar of the generator truck with its broken exhaust system, not to speak of the jungle-like roar of the semi's motor—all would diminish with time.

We made it to Kellogg. This was it. I was super-nervous. I ate another Baby Ruth. I had always hated Baby Ruth candy bars. They looked like eating a turd. Maybe that's how I felt—like eating shit. Not guilty, just low down.

I gave myself instant heartburn and a toothache. The peanuts were stale. Maybe I was making a chocolate and peanut cross for my Golgotha, like Shannon in Tennessee Williams's *Night of the Iguana*—a gawddamned stale cross of junk food to politely martyr myself with.

Most of the Pie Car junk food was gone. I'd be glad when there was no more candy left to be my hemlock.

The hours passed by in agonized slowness, as if to drag the torture out—to drive the crown of thorns deeper. To make matters worse, there were three shows today for Kellogg.

Shadow lifted his long black head and bayed mournfully, but I couldn't hear any siren, not even off in the distance. He dragged his chain back and forth across the metal stair.

Big John arrived minutes after the first show began. But Curtis would run the office until midnight tonight. Then, when they pulled out and got to the fork in the road, the show would go to the left and we would continue on to the right.

Curtis and John talked. He understood. We were leaving peaceably. I was glad for that.

Now the generator had been shut down. The circus moved out of town. Tomorrow—somewhere else—the circus would mushroom up on a vacant lot. Only we would be somewhere else on our way back to California.

We passed Coeur d'Elene—beautiful, misty blue lake surrounded by tall pines, sharp, steep green hills, purple mountains beyond. The shimmering rivers of current, wind-driven, rolling, undulating, reflected the gray clouds above. The air was cooler for last night's rain. The air was moist, pungent with pine. The wind blew the small waves toward shore, toward sailboat-decked inlets, toward coves with tiny brown beaches and deserted boat ramps.

Out on the lake, a sailboat drifted lazily by, its course straight, not tacking back and forth. Beyond, a fisherman slept in a small dinghy, fish laughing at him from beneath the waters.

> There is silence at six A.M.
> Peace on a deserted playing field.
> The circus sleeps like drugged children—
> Their game over until the next show.

The elephant quietly sways,
    The bear moans softly in his cage.
But the small animal noises
    Are swallowed up in the cool morning.
Later, there will be a low hum of activity
    Until the Hey Bey! Hey Bey! is heard
And the tent creaks upward and swells out
    And the chant of labor becomes a cry of victory!
She's up, men! Tent's up!
    Elephant trumpets gloriously.
Another day, another stand,
    A midway full of sticky-faced kids,
Cotton candy smells and popcorn
    And the endless lines of patrons waiting
Circus time! And the parade—
    All the proud little ring ponies,
Going 'round and 'round and 'round,
    Endlessly doing what they have done
        Ten thousand times before.

—Terry Ross Erickson
    "Cookie"

0-595-29641-6

Printed in the United States
24338LVS00005B/98

9 780595 296415